1

WINTER AT CHRISTMAS COTTAGE
DG Valentine

For David and Stuart
Thank you for the inspiration. May Christmas Cottage
one day become a reality!

Chapter 1

Snow fell silently from the night sky and settled on the drifts that surrounded the trees and lined the road. Peace and quiet hung in the air, almost as a nod to the sanctity of the season.

Winter seemed to last forever in the tiny Colorado town of Waybridge. Surrounded by mountains, Waybridge had earned itself the nickname of "The Christmas Town". The residents were all to keen to keep the tradition going and the town was festooned with bright lights and decorations from the beginning of November to mid-January.

The small stone cottage with its peaked roof and arched windows was nestled amid the trees. Situated on the edge of Waybridge, the cottage was connected to the surrounding area by a narrow, winding road. The only indication that anyone was at home was a lamp that lit the road's entrance and a small slate plaque that read *Christmas Cottage*.

The cottage's curtains were closed against the cold, winter night and there was no other signs that anyone was home. Despite Thanksgiving having been only a week previous, there were no decorations and no twinkling lights. Just the heavy sense that the cottage's owner didn't want to be disturbed.

Yet, beyond the heavy wooden door, was a scene of apparent domestic bliss. A fire roared in a wrought iron grate and, even though the cottage was on the utilities, several hurricane lamps threw rays of welcoming yellow light around the small space. The yellow granite walls were hung with paintings and photographs while the dark wooden table was hidden beneath the evidence of a meal enjoyed. A simple brass chandelier hung from the vaulted ceiling and an open plan bedroom could be seen peeking through the beams.

Slumped in a leather chair before the fire, Jay watched as the flames raced up the chimney. With silver hair curling into the nap of his neck and a striped sweater pulled over his portly frame, Jay was the epitome of someone's grandpa. A slate grey cat – Blue – was draped in his lap. Both human and cat appeared to be content and at ease. Yet one of them had thoughts of the upcoming season on their mind.

At fifty-five, Jay had seen a lot of Christmases. Most had been happy. Some... not so much. There had been the ones gathered around the tree with his kids. And the ones where he'd been lost at the bottom of a bottle.

Even so, his first Christmas without his family was going to be hard. Just a year previously, he'd been married with three beautiful children. Then he'd come out of the closet and his world had been shattered. He hadn't spoken to either his ex or his kids in the best part of a year. And now he had to face Christmas, supposedly the most wonderful time of the year, without them.

He couldn't really blame them for leaving. The life that they'd all lead together had been a complete lie. They all thought that they were a happy and healthy family. In reality, they'd smiled for the cameras without knowing the truth that lived deep in Jay's soul.

Jay's hand gently massaged the cat's back as he watched the fire. Logs popped and crackled and the flames gave off the warming glow that he loved so much. While he may have finally have admitted who he was to the world it didn't mean that he wasn't depressed. Not suicidal but definitely feeling the cold pangs of a long winter beginning to pierce his soul.

He'd let his wife and children keep the house. It seemed only fair that they would get the lion's share of what they'd accumulated. He'd consciously lead them on and used them to hide his true self behind. Now it was their turn to live and heal just as it was his time to truly discover who he was.

So Jay had bought a secluded cottage in the mountains. Waybridge was about an hour from his former home and hidden away enough that no one cared who he was or why he was there.

Shortly after moving to the cottage he'd dropped his next bombshell and quit his ridiculously successful band. Formed in 1982, when Jay had been a mere teenager, Winter Angels had gone on to become one of the most successful heavy metal bands to walk the Earth. Everyone wanted to see them and all were willing to pay over the odds to get tickets. But Jay had had enough; he'd accumulated enough money for himself, his family, and the next generations of his family to never have to worry. He'd wanted out of the music business for a long time and had finally found the perfect excuse to make his escape. So he'd turned and walked, leaving Mitch, the drummer, Rob, the lead guitarist, and Tim, the bass player, completely in the lurch. They'd obviously not agreed with and had begged him to stay. But there was no changing Jay's mind; he'd put down his guitar and gone in the hope of building a brand new life away from the chaos that he'd endured since his late-teens.

Another log popped and Jay managed a soft smile as he slumped lower in the deep chair. Blue only purred louder as though he knew that they were in for a long evening of sitting and staring at the fire.

Chapter 2

Mondays were trivia night at Joe's Java Shack. Nestled at the top of Waybridge's Main Street, Joe's was a snug coffee shop that was haunted by many of the locals, particularly those who wanted to escape from the tourist traps of the bars and restaurants.

From the week before Thanksgiving to when the snows melted in April, Waybridge was packed with tourists. All of them came to ski, snowboard, or admire the picturesque European-style town with its wood-and-stone buildings, unique stores, world class food, and, of course, its award-winning Christmas decorations. The locals had a chance to catch their breath in May before the summer tourists began to pile in. May was when Jay had most felt at peace. The lack of people meant that there was less chance of him being commandeered for photos and autographs.

Tucked in the snug beside the open fire, Jay could watch people coming and going. While he didn't take part in the trivia evenings, he enjoyed the social aspect of being surrounded by people. Even if it was only once a week, it was good for him to get out of the house and to temporarily stop brooding on whether he truly was living life his way.

Fairy lights twinkled in the coffee shop's rafters and an oversized Christmas tree decorated with more lights and sparkling baubles was nestled beside the door. Soft Christmas music played in the background and Jay felt oddly at peace with himself. He may not have been celebrating the holiday in the traditional sense but he was celebrating.

An old thrift store paperback rested on his lap and a mug of the shop's home brew sat on the low, beat-up coffee table. The shop really was his kind of place; laid back, easy going and with no pressure to join in.

Jay's eyes drifted to the counter in the furthest corner of the shop. There was no way he couldn't look as the person standing at the counter was waving their arms around, presumably as they tried to describe a drink. From the corner of his eye, he noticed several other people also watching. By the look on the barista's face, whoever was ordering wasn't a regular.

His attention finally drifted back to his book and he snuggled down into the overstuffed armchair. The crackling of the fire and the gentle music mixed with the rich smell of coffee forced Jay to relax and focus on something other than himself.

"Mind if I sit here?"

The voice was male and oddly gentle. Glancing up from the book, Jay found himself looking at the man from the counter. He was dressed head to foot in black; black jeans, black hoodie, and a pair of black rimmed glasses on his nose. Long dark hair curled around his shoulders and a neatly trimmed beard framed his soft smile.

Jay looked around the busy coffee shop and found that the only seat was the easy chair beside him.

Everyone and his Momma in this bitch tonight. Trivia night isn't normally this busy.

Finally, Jay shrugged and nodded. "Sure."

The man's smile widened and he dropped himself into the seat. He took a sip of his drink before placing it on the table. Letting his shoulders drop back to the chair, Jay turned his attention back to his book.

"What are you reading?"

He frowned and peered up at the man. "Sorry?"

The man tucked a handful of stray hairs behind his ear before nodding to the book in Jay's lap.

"Oh. This?" Jay lifted the book for the man to see. He watched, fascinated, as man tilted his head before squinting and pushing the glasses further up his nose.

"*A Brief History of Denver.* Sounds riveting," the man drily added before holding his hand out. "Dominic."

Dropping a bookmark into the open pages, Jay closed the book before taking the offered hand. "Jay. You always this chatty, Dominic?"

Dominic flashed him another of those bright, million watt smiles. "Yeah, I am. How's life without Winter Angels?"

Jay struggled to not roll his eyes. *Yay. Here we go.* He had absolutely zero desire to talk about his previous life, his music, nor the alcohol fuelled lifestyle that had lead him to falling off the face of the entertainment industry and shacking up in Colorado.

"Good," he replied. "Really good. I'm really enjoying my downtime." He quickly changed the subject. "What do you do, Dominic?"

The dark haired man gestured to the street beyond the windows. "I run a store just down the street. Between the Sheets. It's a sheet music store that I opened three months ago."

"You from the area?" Jay placed the book on the table and picked up his coffee. It was no use trying to look as though he was ignoring Dominic. If he did,

Dominic would just butt into his quiet time. *May as well play along for the minute.*

"Nah. Virginia originally. Lived in LA for the past twenty years, though. I'd forgotten how cold, and cut off, it can be living in a place like Waybridge." Dominic gave him another smile, one that was warm and endearing and filled with hope. "You should come by the store sometime."

Jay shook his head. "I'm taking a break. I don't even have a guitar here with me."

He really didn't want to be talking. He wanted to be alone in his own bubble and undisturbed by outside forces like human interaction.

But his therapist had told him that being a permanent hermit wasn't good for his health especially if he wanted to back into music at some point. Being around other people would help when he finally decided to what he was going to do. *If* he decided go back.

"Well, come by and talk, even if it's not about music," Dominic earnestly pressed.

Jay fiddled with the mug in his hands, desperate for the interaction to end. "Yeah, I'll think about it."

"You doing the quiz?"

Glancing away from Dominic, Jay spotted Eric, the quiz-master, wandering between tables and handing out answer sheets. "Wasn't planning on it. Was just planning on having a cup of coffee and reading my book."

There was an impish sparkle to Dominic's eyes. "Come on! It'll be fun."

He could hear his therapist's voice in his head.

Could hear the words that had been repeated so often over the course of so many sessions. *Human interaction, Jay. You need it a minimum of twice a week even if it's just buying your groceries or going to the coffee shop. Next time we talk, I want to hear about at least one conversation that you've had. And not just you asking your cat what he wanted for dinner.*

When Eric passed by, Jay reached up and took an answer sheet. The young man looked down at him and raised an eyebrow. Eric knew all too well that Jay had his rituals and none of them included quiz night. Jay just gave him a crooked smile.

❅❅❅

"Looks like we've won a dinner for two at Stone Bridge Inn."

Jay stared at Dominic's grinning face and frowned. He couldn't believe that they'd entered and somehow come second. Unfortunately, Dominic's knowledge of pop trivia had sent them storming to the top of the leader table before Jay's own knowledge of 1990s lyrics had sent them slithering back down.

"You use it," he mumbled.

"And take who?" Dominic countered. "I don't know anyone in Waybridge. Except for my landlord and I doubt that he'll take this as payment on my rent. Looks like it's you and me, Hammond."

Sweeping his eyes up and down Dominic's plump body, Jay had to bite back a *Looks like you could manage two meals.* The man obviously ate well but

16

then Jay was in no place to criticise. With a paunch gently resting on the waistband of his jeans, his own body showed signs of a life well lived. Instead, he stood and gathered up his coat and book. He'd come out of the closet and hadn't so much as touched another man. It still felt... wrong and oddly against the morals that had been instilled in him. And he didn't want to start with Dominic. He didn't know why, he just didn't.

"Night, Dominic. Sleep well."

Fuck. A pair of dark doe eyes stared back up at him and Jay felt the guilt begin to eat away at him. Dominic wanted a friend and someone to talk to. He was desperately lonely while Jay was desperate to be left alone.

His shoulders slumped beneath his thick winter coat. "I'll swing by the shop tomorrow."

It was a hollow promise but it made Dominic smile.

"Okay. We'll make a date for dinner then."

Jay rolled his eyes as he turned to leave. "No. We won't."

❄❄❄

Being raised by Christian parents meant that Christian guilt and Christian morals often racked Jay's thoughts. Homosexuality didn't exist in their world. It was an abomination. A sin. Something that was never spoken about. And it didn't matter that some branches of the church were now accepting people like himself. The guilt still lived on, slowly rotting his soul. No matter how much therapy he had, Jay couldn't erase the sense that he was in the wrong. He loved his wife and adored his children. But there was a deeper part of him that was unfulfilled. And it was that part that he was desperately trying to come to terms with.

His feet crunched over freshly fallen snow and snowflakes whispered passed his ears. Twinkling lights were strung across Waybridge's Main Street and every window was bright with decorations and Christmas promises. But his mind, as always, was fighting with itself. His heart wanted one thing but his mind wanted something completely different.

He took a left just before the bridge and stepped into the forest. Leaving the festive lights of the town behind, Jay climbed among the trees. The silence was a welcome respite from the noise of the evening. Dominic's voice still rattled around his head, whispering answers to him or confirming what he'd already written down. If he closed his eyes, Jay could see the other man leaning closer. Could smell the musky scent of his cologne. Could feel the ends of that dark hair brushing against his cheek.

The silence of the trees was broken by his breath catching sharply in his throat. Leaning against an ice-speckled trunk, Jay stared up into the darkness ahead of him. He couldn't allow himself to get caught up in such thoughts. Dominic wasn't – and would never be – his type. The high energy, constantly talking man would eventually end up irritating him. And Jay dared not think of what would happen when that moment arrived.

On top of all of that, Dominic was a fan. And

dating fans went against everything he believed in. He wanted someone calm and collected who would love him for all of his quirks. That's if he ever found anyone. Breaking down the barriers that had been built up throughout his life was taking more work than he'd anticipated. When he'd first come out of the closet, Jay had believed that he could happily skip into the first gay venue he came across and pick someone up.

Except it wasn't as easy as that. Nothing in his life was ever that easy. Guys looked at him as though he was some kind of freak. Firstly, he was *old*. And old came with its own stereotypes, all of which required experience and of which he had none. No one wanted to even look out at a fresh out of the closet guy with grey hair and a heavy stomach. And that was the second thing. He just didn't look right. The first, and only place, that he'd hit up had a distinct lack of body shapes. Everyone, bar himself, had been painfully young and slender.

The experience had sent Jay fleeing back to the safety of the hotel he'd been living in. Unable to bear the thought of trying to learn how to live in his new world, Jay had done what he'd always done and cut himself off. He spoke to no one, saw no one, and refused to even acknowledge the presence of the band that he'd been a part of for so many years. As far as he was concerned, he was a non-person and he didn't want anyone to see him.

Listening to the sounds of the forest, he took a moment to compose himself. Somewhere a clump of snow fell from a branch. An owl called out. In the distance the river could be heard trickling beneath the bridge.

Above the trees was the road that wound its way around Waybridge. The narrow paved track that lead to his house cut away from the road before winding its way through the trees and to the wonderfully hidden cottage. Home. A place to rest his head and escape from the noise of the world. A place for him to lick his wounds and attempt, albeit badly, to adapt to the world that he'd put himself into.

Opening the door, Jay was greeted by the warmth of the fire and the glow of the lamps. Turning on the lights seemed fruitless in winter and he found it better to hunker down by the light of the fire. He hadn't got one foot through the door before Blue was winding around his ankles and making his presence known. Smiling, Jay slid his coat and gloves off and reached down to pick the cat up.

"Hey," he murmured. "Had a good evening? Done a lot of sleeping in front of the fire?"

The cat only purred louder and squirmed as Jay walked towards his seat. Dropping himself into it, he gave Blue a squeeze before resting the cat on his lap. Jay could reach over him and undo his walking boots before kicking them away to dry before the fire.

For a while he just stared at the fire, lost in the flicker of the flames and the crackle of the logs. The movement was mesmerising and meditative and allowed him to drift away from the problems that constantly plagued his mind. They were, of course, problems of his own making. Problems that were either very real or very imagined.

He could see himself back in the coffee shop, sitting beside the fire and sipping coffee as he hunched over the quiz sheets. In that moment he'd felt strangely wanted and accepted. Dominic had known who he was but had treated him as an equal, someone to sit and shoot the breeze with while drinking coffee and answering trivia questions. Looking back on it, Jay realised that he shouldn't have been so abrupt with Dominic. Dominic originally hadn't wanted anything from him other the only open seat in a very busy coffee house. Instead, as per usual, Jay had tried to shut out the only person who'd chosen to talk to him that day.

"Stupid fucker," he murmured to himself. Blue flicked an ear. Jay reached down and rested his hand on the cat's back. "I gotta get out of this funk, Blue. Gotta get past all of those walls I've built round myself. Otherwise I'm never gonna get anywhere and I'll spend the rest of my life stuck in this house." Jay sighed and sank a little lower into the seat. "Not that fading away here is a bad thing but I came out of the closet for a reason. I was tired of lying to myself. And I'm only fooling myself if I don't want to explore that, right?"

Again, Blue flicked his ears and Jay smiled softly. "Ah, to be a cat and only have to think of keeping warm and being fed. But you're a good friend and I appreciate your presence. Thanks for sticking around through all of this."

❊ ❊ ❊

The bed felt as though it was shaking. Clutching his pillows to his head, Jay groaned and tried to roll away from the motion. Instead the sensation got stronger. They didn't live in an earthquake zone so...

Opening an eye, Jay found Blue sitting beside his head. The purring became louder when the cat saw that he'd finally woken. Glancing past his cat, Jay looked at the bedside clock.

9am.

It was no wonder Blue had been trying to wake him. Shuffling closer, he pressed a kiss to the cat's head.

"Sorry, buddy. I must have needed the sleep. How long have you been trying to wake me?"

He reached out and scratched Blue's head, smiling tiredly as the cat kneaded at the bed covers. Sliding from the bed, Jay shoved his feet into slippers and fought his way into a hoodie. Sunbeams could be seen glistening from the snow outside and an icicle as long as his arm dangled precariously above the window.

The oak stairs creaked as he made his way to the kitchen. Nestled at the back of the cottage, it had just enough room for him to make a meal. Buying a small house had been a deliberate move. Jay didn't want to take a lot of his old life with him and less room meant less temptation to take any crap with him. The cottage was open plan with a bathroom positioned beside the balcony-bedroom. The previous owners had fitted out the cottage with beautiful modern appliances so Jay had just had to grab some thrift store furniture and move in. The one thing that he had splashed money on had been a decent bed. Following his divorce, sleep had become a blessing that he didn't want to miss out on.

Once Blue had been fed, Jay made himself a coffee and leaned against the kitchen's porthole window. The garden was piled high with snow and wouldn't be fully visible until at least the middle of February. He was looking forward to getting outside and tending to the tiny piece of land. It had been overgrown with waist high grass when he'd moved in and Fall had come and gone by the time he'd finished clearing it. The garden was now tidy, albeit snow-blocked, and Jay was hoping to do something with it. Maybe a vegetable patch or some flowers.

As he watched misty-grey clouds roll around the mountains, his mind drifted to the previous night. True to his word, Jay barely knew anyone in Waybridge and was adamant about keeping himself to himself. Years of lawyers and therapists and bumbled attempts at rehab had left him with a distinct distaste in his mouth about being around people, especially for extended periods of time. He didn't want anyone else meddling in his life, just the peace and quiet of the mountains and the company of his cat.

That's not to say that he didn't miss his ex-wife. Jay had been the first to admit that he'd married her under false pretences. He'd been trying to hide from his true self, denying a crucial part of his identity and forcing it into hiding for so many years. The whole issue had finally boiled over during one of his many therapy sessions. His sexuality had been nagging at him for the best part of a decade and he'd started drinking in order to try and quieten it. Which had resulted in him going on daily benders, crashing a car, ending up in hospital, and having to cancel a year's worth of tour dates. The ultimatum had come from management: Rehab or the band ends.

So he'd reluctantly gone to rehab and confessed everything. They'd suggested marriage therapy. Which was when Jay had come out to the woman who'd spent nearly thirty years believing she was married to a heterosexual man. The divorce papers had, almost wisely, been delivered while he was still in treatment.

Ragged and a little raw, Jay had been released back into the world after three months of being locked in an in-patient facility. With no home to go back to, he'd collected what he believed he'd needed and found Christmas Cottage. Arrangements had been made for everything else that he owned to go into storage. He was dead to his wife and Jay couldn't blame her. A quarter of her life was a long time to live a lie.

The kids were all in their twenties and able to make their own decisions. There was no custody battle to be fought, just the hope that, one day, they'd want to see their father again.

Jay could see is ghostly reflection in the frost-etched window. His hair – once sun-blonde – was now silver and curled down into his neck. His body, once tall and slender, now carried the weight of many hours of comfort eating. His sky-blue eyes stared back at him, taking in the man that he'd become. And Jay wasn't sure if he liked himself. He was a freshly-out-of-the-closet gay man with no experience in the LGBT world. He'd only known how to pick up woman and his thoughts from the previous night, the thoughts of trying to pick up a man, nagged at him like a stuck record.

Jay downed his rapidly cooling coffee and left the mug beside the sink. He needed groceries and, with his license still suspended for the next year, that meant walking everywhere.

Chapter 3

"Jay? Jay?! *Jay?!*"

Screwing his eyes closed, Jay dropped his head and continued walking. He didn't want to be disturbed while out shopping. He just wanted to get what he needed and go home.

Fuck off, Dominic.

Jay continued to walk as he ignored the muffled apologies as the man from the night before dodged around tourists. Waybridge, as per usual for the time of the year, was busy with visitors. Crowds mingled on the wide cobbled street, taking photographs and looking in the various stores. Above them, the blue sky shimmered with watery-winter sun.

"Sorry. 'scuse me. Sorry. Coming through. Sorry."

Jay could hear laboured breathing and feet crunching over freshly-salted cobbles. Finally Dominic pulled up beside him, his face flushed red and his chest heaving as he gasped for breath.

"I was yelling you, man," he muttered.

He gave Dominic an apologetic smile. "Sorry. Didn't hear you."

Dominic placed a hand on his arm in order to stop him and Jay found himself taking a reactionary step back. People were always trying to touch him. They wanted hugs and kisses and everything in between. But having them so close made him feel uncomfortable. He loved the people who wanted to express their gratitude but he didn't particularly love their ways of showing affection. It took him a second to realise that Dominic wanted him to stop in order to catch his breath.

Leaning forward, Dominic rested his hands on his knees and drew in a handful of shaking breaths. "I saw you walking past the store and thought I'd see if you'd made your mind up about that meal."

With his long hair whipping around his face and his dark eyes full of hope, Jay couldn't help but feel something for Dominic.

He placed a hand on the other man's shoulder. "Dominic, it's a sweet gesture. But, like I said last night, find someone else to take. Besides, I don't go out with fans." Jay gave him an apologetic shrug. "Sorry. Personal policy."

Heartbreak and sadness seared across Dominic's face and Jay felt himself standing on the brink of collapse. Oh, how he wanted *some* human interaction. But he'd hoped that it wouldn't be with someone as boisterous as Dominic.

Dominic brushed a handful of hair from his face and began walking back to his store. Jay could feel the other man's pain and see the heaviness in his steps. How often had he been the one who'd been rejected? With ten albums and numerous awards to his band's name, rejection, and the inevitable agony, didn't happen much any more. Fame and celebrity status saw that he had everything he'd ever need. But when he'd been younger... The rejection, and those dragging footsteps, had been a daily occurrence. Dominic didn't want to impose on his life. Dominic wanted a friend. And, no matter how much he protested, Jay needed people around.

Don't do it. You were going to the supermarket,

dumbass. Go after him and he'll never leave.

Jay took a step forward and held up a gloved hand. "Dominic, wait."

Don't say I didn't warn you.

Falling into step beside Dominic, Jay gave the still crestfallen man a soft smile. Those eyes, as dark as the night sky, still swam with an ocean of pain and that cheery smile had faded to nothing.

"I said I'd come and see your shop," he softly said.

"But you all but told me to fuck off," Dominic protested. "I get it, Jay. Don't take pity on me. Like you said, I'm "just a fan" and you don't fraternise with fans. I get it. I doubt I would hang out with the likes of me if I was in your position."

That was a knife to the heart. A cold, sharp knife that Dominic had thrust in as hard as he could and twisted until Jay's blood ran cold. Once upon a time, his fighting instinct would have kicked in and he'd have given Dominic a mouthful of abuse before storming off. But he was now older and wiser and understood Dominic's anger.

"I'm not," he softly replied. "I really do want to see it. I miss music." Jay sighed and stuffed his hands in pockets. His eyes drifted to the trees that dotted the street. Their bare branches were decorated with lights and elegant decorations. There was nothing but the best in Waybridge. "Music is the friend that doesn't leave when the going gets tough. Only I was the one to walk out on music and it's time to see if it'll have me back."

Dominic seemed to relax a little and Jay couldn't blame him for being on guard. He'd given the other man several excuses as to why they couldn't get to know one another before doing a complete one-eighty and demanding Dominic's attention.

"I hear you," Dominic replied. "Come on in. The heating's on at least."

With his hands still stuffed in his pockets, Jay followed Dominic as they weaved in and out of the mid-day crowds. A bell tinkled above the door as they walked in and Jay was immediately hit by the relaxing scent of ageing paper. Books of music and loose leaf sheets were neatly sorted onto dark wooden shelves. Like every other store on the street, the ceiling was bare and stripped back to its beams and rafters. Light-bulbs artfully dangled from the beams and threw pools of warm light around the small space. A desk and cash register were set up at the far end of the shop and, true to his word, the heating was chasing away the biting mountain winter.

"Welcome to Between the Sheets," Dominic said with a warm smile. "There's music for every instrument and every genre. Want old sheet music for art projects? It's in the basket by the window. Gifts for your musically inclined friends? They're by the register."

Dominic's excitement was infectious and Jay couldn't help but return his smile. "This place is amazing! You've done a great job."

"Thanks." Dominic shrugged his coat off and tossed it on a nearby chair. "Coffee?"

"I'd love one, thanks."

Once Dominic had disappeared out the back of the shop, Jay took to exploring the small room. His

29

fingers wandered over both old and new books, pulling them out in order to examine the notes which danced across the pages. Dominic hadn't been lying; the shop really did contain everything. From the old masters to current bands, Dominic truly had thought of everything.

He walked between the shelves and the counter, carefully piling books onto the varnished surface. By the time Dominic returned, Jay had selected ten that he wanted. There was no harm having music in the cottage despite his lack of piano or guitar. It would be there if he ever needed and would act as another reassurance in a world that was feeling increasingly hostile to him.

"Woah! Dude!" Dominic eyed the pile of books as he put the mugs down. "I'll give you a discount on those."

The smile was suddenly permanently etched onto Jay's face. He shook his head. "You know who I am so you know that I'm good for the cash."

Dominic silently looked at him for a moment, obviously taking in what Jay had said. After what seemed like an eternity, Dominic began to total the books.

"Two hundred and forty-eight dollars. Jay..."

Knowing what Dominic was going to say about how much he was spending, Jay silently handed over his credit card. The piece of plastic was taken from him and swiped. He scrawled his signature on the receipt and handed it back. Dominic looked at it before carefully placing it in the till.

"Gonna frame that," he said whimsically. "Jay

Hammond bought books from me."

Dominic's child-like admiration of the tiny piece of paper melted a little of Jay's heart. Dominic seemed both naïve and worldly as though he had a foot in both worlds and walked a line that only he could see. It was his turn to be quiet as he watched Dominic lift his head and stare at him with a faraway look in his eyes. Jay felt something wrap around his chest and hold him tight, a warmth that he was only just noticing. Something else churned and fluttered in his stomach, swimming through him and sparking flares of happiness.

"Dominic." He kept his voice low so as not to break the tranquil moment. "Let's make a date for that meal."

Dominic's smile widened into all of its beautiful glory. "When are you free?"

"Every night of the week. I live a solitary life but my therapist tells me that I need to have human contact at least twice a week. You can be the human contact I tell him about." Jay gave him another smile. "He'll think I'm a different person when I tell him that I had dinner with someone."

The other man's laughter was gentle and warm and filled the tiny shop with sound. Dominic genuinely seemed like a joy to be around and Jay was glad that he was managing to see through his own idiocy. Jay was determined to push through his self imposed policies and limitations. Sure, he'd put them in place for a reason but sometimes he had to push himself to break with policy and procedure and try to enjoy life. And that was one of the reasons that he'd come out of the closet in the first place.

"How's Tuesday night? I keep the shop open late on weekends for the tourists. And you seem well known in the coffee shop on a Monday-"

"Mandatory human contact," Jay jokingly interjected. "Next Tuesday it is. I'll put it on my overflowing calendar."

There was more laughter from the dark haired man and Jay was happy at how easily Dominic laughed. Happiness was something that was missing in his life and he needed to get it back in somehow or another. Apparently it seemed that his happiness was going to return thanks to the man who ran the music shop.

"Tuesday night, 7pm?"

Jay peered over the top of his mug. "Sounds good. Get it booked, Dominic."

❄❄❄

For the next hour, they drank coffee and chatted back and forth. As promised, Dominic didn't talk exclusively about music. Instead he regaled Jay with with tales of his life, of trying to make it in the Hollywood music scene, of setting up a barbecuing business in his forties and selling it when he hit fifty. Then he'd decided that he wanted out of the city but didn't want to move back to Virginia. So he'd Googled "America's Most Picturesque Towns" and landed in Waybridge. Dominic had used the money from the sale of his company to lease the shop and set up Between the Sheets.

"So what about you?" Dominic finally asked.

"You're not a local. What bought you here?"

Glancing into his now-empty mug, Jay tried to read the dregs of the coffee for a sign. Tell all? Or lie?

"Want the truth?"

He saw Dominic nod and, taking a deep breath, Jay began, "I came out of the closet after living a lie for my whole life. My wife divorced me and I wanted nothing more than to be out of her hair. I wanted to be away from people and be a hermit. You know about Winter Angels, Dominic." Jay shrugged. "I've always been a bit of an introvert. But you'd only have heard what they would have said on TMZ; that I'd been to rehab – true, by the way – and wanted time away from the band."

Dominic's face was a picture of shock and the dark-haired man murmured a soft, "Wow."

Jay nodded before placing his empty mug on the counter. "And that's how I ended up in Waybridge."

The bell above the door tinkled and he watched Dominic look up. Sensing a shift in the atmosphere, Jay picked up the paper bag that the dark-haired man had packed his books in.

"I'll see you later, Dominic. Thanks for the coffee and the conversation. I really appreciate it."

The other man straightened up as someone walked around the shop. His dark eyes finally returned to Jay's and there was a ghost of a smile on his lips. "Don't forget to tell your therapist about your human interaction."

Jay chuckled and shook his head. "Cheeky fucker."

❊ ❊ ❊

The grocery store, aptly named The Waybridge General Store, was at the top of Main Street, just past the coffee shop and right before Tiny Treasures. Tiny Treasures, as the name suggested, stocked tiny replicas of the landmarks, most mountains, ski resorts, and Waybridge's famous stone bridge.

For a tourist town, the store was surprisingly well stocked. Christmas music bubbled from hidden speakers and bright lights illuminated the produce. One aisle was dedicated to holiday treats. Jay tried to avoid that aisle. His waist line liked to expand especially around the holiday season. Instead, he picked up vegetables, chicken, and some fresh pasta. Salami, one of Blue's favourite snacks, also made its way into the basket.

The store only had four check-outs and all of them were manned. Customers, both locals and tourists, lined up to buy their day's groceries. Jay knew that he needed to start stocking up as the coming weeks would become busier as they closed in on Christmas. And he really didn't want to be in the town centre when the hordes descended in those final, futile hours before the clock struck midnight and Christmas Day arrived.

"Morning, Mr Hammond."

Jay was snapped out of his thoughts and found himself looking at Diego, one of the store's young clerks. While Jay had kept himself away from the adult population of Waybridge, the younger generation had gone out of their way to make him feel welcome. Jay couldn't find it in himself to turn them

34

away. Instead, he was endeared by how they made conversation about anything but his private life and band. More human contact for him. But happy human contact. They would talk about school, skiing, their pets and, in turn, would ask how he was finding Waybridge and about his cat. They weren't prying into his personal life and Jay adored them for it.

He paid for his groceries and packed them into the cotton bag that he'd pulled from his pocket. The street outside was full of people admiring the scenery. Waybridge was perched on the side of a mountain and, across the river, the rest of the range swept upwards into the snowy-sky. Swathes of fir trees marched along the ridges, their branches stark against the slate grey of the mountains. It truly was a breath-taking sight and Jay hoped to never tire of it.

Chapter 4

The days until the meal with Dominic flew by. Waybridge was officially on countdown to Christmas and the tiny town became a veritable metropolis as everyone from the surrounding area crammed into the streets to see the lights, buy gifts, and be merry.

But there would be no Christmas at Christmas Cottage. It was just another day on the calendar. Jay had already had his small selection of festive treats, a tin of nice cocoa, and a handful of battered thrift store paperbacks. There was a small box of treats for Blue and the pair of them would spend the day beside a roaring fire. No one from his previous life knew where he was so there would be no cards that he felt obliged to reply to and no unexpected visitors. All in all it was set to be a lovely, and peaceful, day.

Jay looked at himself in the closet mirror. He'd ditched the jeans and baggy sweatshirts and opted instead for grey suit pants and a white shirt topped off with a grey vest. The cold would be fought off with a fleece lined suit jacket.

Getting to Stone Bridge Inn would be an issue so Jay called the local cab company and, at 6.30pm precisely, a black car pulled onto his narrow drive. Taking a deep breath, he kissed the cat and let himself out. His heart fluttered as he climbed into the back of the car and he gave his perfect little house one last glance as they pulled out onto the road.

The ride was short but Jay found himself going over a myriad of situations. Would Dominic stand him up? Would they actually have anything in common?

And why was he worrying? It wasn't like he was actually going on a date. They'd won a meal and it would be a crime to let it go to waste. But did Dominic see it as a date? And if he did, why? Jay didn't even know if the dark-haired man swung his way.

Stone Bridge Inn was, as the name suggested, a restaurant that sat beside the town's picturesque bridge. The restaurant featured open plan dining, bare walls and beams, and plenty of ambiance. Jay found himself being seated in a little nook with what would, in daylight. be a view of the river. Candles burned on the table, throwing warm shadows around the small space. He perused the menu as he waited, eyeing up both the pasta and the steak. It had been a while since he'd last eaten anything that took more than a single pan to cook.

Jay waited.

And waited.

And waited.

He started a tab for drinks. Water and soda in his case but it was there if Dominic wanted anything different.

He waited some more, his heart aching as he looked around himself. Dominic had done what Jay had thought he'd do and stood him up. With a sigh, Jay picked up the menu and was about to get the waiter's attention when a shadowy figure walked up to the table. Jay looked up and had to stifle a gasp.

Lit by the soft candle-light was Dominic. He was dressed in his customary black but had switched the jeans for suit pants and the t-shirt for a button down shirt. The ensemble was topped off with a black suit jacket that hugged the lines of Dominic's body. His hair had lost its ratty, wind-blown look and instead sat around his shoulder in thick, shiny waves. The scent of something with notes of vanilla and musk gently drifted around the space as Dominic moved to sit.

"Sorry I'm late." Dominic's voice was painfully gentle and almost nervous. "I lost track of time at the shop. Then the car wouldn't start."

"Well, you're here. And I'm glad that you're here. What would you like to drink?"

Dominic toyed with the cuffs of his jacket, his gaze never on Jay. "Just a soda."

"Sure? You can have something else," Jay offered. "I'm not going to be offended."

Waves of dark hair fell into Dominic's face as he shook his head. The eyes that eventually looked at Jay were wide and filled with a sadness that he related to.

"A soda's fine. I kinda-" Dominic sighed and once more hid his face from view. Jay watched as he took off his glasses and rubbed the bridge of his nose. "I've kinda been hitting the bottle and I need to slow down. The winter months are getting to me more than I thought they would."

Jay felt himself soften and warm a little more to the man before him. "It's okay. You can talk."

"I don't want to ruin the evening," Dominic quietly protested.

"You're not, I promise."

Dominic sighed and was silent before picking up his glasses. "Being here reminds me of why I moved away from Virginia. The winters were killer and I get depressed really quickly. I thought the shop would be a distraction but it's not. Not as much as I wanted it to be. Can we talk about something else, please?"

Resting his elbows on the table, Jay gazed through the flickering candle to Dominic. "Of course we can. Like what we're going to eat."

Dominic's face broke into a smile at the mention of food and Jay handed him a menu. As Dominic began to relax, so they began to talk; about their lives, about their families, about their hobbies. Jay talked about restoring old cars while Dominic waxed lyrical about the perfect barbecue. They only paused to place their orders - T-bone for Jay and porterhouse steak for Dominic – before diving right back in.

And Jay found something really weird happening. He found himself liking Dominic and relating to him. Dominic may been a Winter Angels fan on the surface but, beneath all of that, there was a whole lot more to him. Dominic wasn't trying to be his buddy because of who Jay was. He genuinely wanted a friend and to be someone to another person.

"How's it going with the band?" Dominic finally asked.

Jay tried not to grit his teeth and merely nodded. Hell, in the form of Mitch, had blown in when Jay had first announced his intention to leave. Mitch had been the primary driving force behind the band and had helped them climb from dirty teenage rockers to screaming stadium superstars. But, as the dust had settled, everyone had realised that Jay leaving for a while was for the best. Rehab, divorce, and coming out of the closet needed time to be processed and it was easier for them all to spend time apart. At least for a while.

"It's going as well as it can," he replied. "We're on hiatus for now. But I'm sure we'll get back together at some point. It was tough walking away, don't get me wrong. But I had to do it for my own sanity. I miss them all but I know that I'll see them again."

Dominic was sombre for a moment and Jay wondered if he'd upset the other man. He glanced down at his drink and toyed with the heavy base of the glass. The light-hearted atmosphere had changed to something heavier. Unspoken words hung between them, waiting patiently in the wings to make themselves known.

It was Dominic who spoke first, "Even if you don't go back, you've left a huge legacy. All that music, all that emotion. It's timeless, Jay."

Jay felt a smile begin to tug at his lips. Looking up, he found Dominic looking at him with those gentle eyes. Worry swam through them and Jay wondered who he was nervous for. Dominic's hand was wrapped around his glass, his knuckles white. Reaching out, Jay touched a finger to the back of Dominic's hand.

"Drink up, Dominic. Get some sugar in you. I want to see the happy, hyper you again."

❄ ❄ ❄

Dinner was, as Jay expected, delicious. Happy Dominic returned, only to lustily moan over his meal. The man really was a foodie and so Jay found himself warming a little more to the dark-haired man.

When the time came for them to leave, Jay felt full, both physically and spiritually. He wasn't going to lie; for all his reservations he'd really enjoyed Dominic's company.

"Where's your car?" Dominic asked.

Embarrassed, Jay shoved his hands into his pockets. "My license is still suspended. My house isn't far from here so I'll walk."

"I'll give you a ride if you like."

He really didn't want the night to end. Which seemed an odd concept to Jay. He'd always wanted his own company and no one else's. Getting married had been part and parcel of life and he'd accepted all that his wife had been. On top of that, he truly had loved her and, thankfully, she'd understood his need to be alone.

More snow was forecast and, as much as he enjoyed a walk in the darkness, Jay decided to lean on the side of caution.

"Sure. A ride would be appreciated. Thanks."

He allowed Dominic to lead him around the property and to the parking lot at the rear. They wound their way through the rows of cars until they reached a small red hatchback. Jay raised an eyebrow and, in the low light from the restaurant's windows, he watched Dominic shrug.

"It's nippy. That's all I need around here. Besides, the roads I use are always clear so..."

Jay glanced back to the car and took in its tiny statue. "The access road to mine isn't clear. You might get it on and off. But there's room to park on the main road. Besides, I'll be getting straight out."

Dominic's expression fell a little and Jay felt his resolve once more begin to crumble.

"Or you could come and grab a coffee before you head on home."

That smile returned, tugging at the corners of the other man's lips and transforming his face into a beacon of light. Chuckling quietly, Jay shook his head and sat himself in the car. Dominic was a character, seemingly part man and part boy, always in search of some kind of attention or affection. Not that Jay could blame him. Dominic had admitted that the winter had hit him hard. It had hit all of them hard. So what if he was allowing Dominic into his house? It was only for a short time and kindness deserved to be rewarded.

❄❄❄

By some kind of magical force, Dominic managed to get the tiny car onto the narrow driveway. Jay was completely baffled by how the other man had managed to navigate nearly a foot of snow until he remembered that Dominic was originally from Virginia. He'd probably driven rot-boxes in far worse conditions.

Jay really wasn't built for tiny cars and he groaned as he unfolded his long legs into the snow. Behind him, feet crunched through the powdery downfall and he could hear Dominic breathing.

"So this is your house, huh?"

Despite the darkness, he turned and smiled at Dominic. "This it is."

"Your cat's waiting for you."

Turning back to the house, Jay spotted Blue sitting in the window. The single lamp that he'd left lit glittered from the cat's grey fur. As per usual, Blue was meowing.

"Yeah," Jay replied with a grin. "It's only because he hasn't been fed for three hours. Come on in and you can meet him. He's a real people cat so he'd like to – yeah – make a new friend." He shrugged as he felt around for his keys.

Jay didn't bother to wait for Dominic. The air was frigid and the promise of more snow hung in the night sky. Sliding the key into the lock, he turned to see if Dominic had followed. Almost puppy-like, the other man was already standing behind him. The porch light caught the waves of Dominic's hair and painted galaxies among the strands.

It was Dominic's next question that caused Jay to stall in getting them both into the warmth.

"If your home is called Christmas Cottage why don't you have decorations up?"

His heart pounded at Dominic's words and Jay guiltily looked down at his shoes. "Because I don't feel up to it this year. Sorry."

You don't have anything to apologise for.

Dominic shrugged. "Fair enough."

The other man's easy acceptance warmed Jay and he gave Dominic a small, tight smile. Pushing the door open, he sighed happily as the heat of the fire raced out and washed over them. From the window, Jay heard a *meow.*

"Welcome to my humble abode," he softly said.

He could hear Dominic walking behind him, his

feet thudding quietly against the stone floor. Something furry wrapped around his ankles and Jay bent down to pick up Blue. The cat wasted no time in settling down and purring up a storm, although Jay could see that one amber eye was cracked open enough to see their guest.

"Blue, this is Dominic. Just be your usual charming self, okay?"

The cat purred a little louder and stretched out his head when Dominic reached to stroke him.

"He's lovely."

"He's a sweetheart," Jay replied. "Best cat I've ever had and been through thick and thin with me over the past few years."

They walked through the cottage and to the kitchen, Blue purring away and Dominic commenting on the beauty of the tiny space.

"Sure is better than my apartment."

Placing the cat on the floor, Jay set the coffee machine running. He found two mugs, one with a slight chip in the rim, and set them beside the machine.

"You live above the shop, right?" he asked.

"Yeah." Dominic was leaning against the faux-marble counter and, to Jay, appeared to surreptitiously take everything in. "I mean, it's great. But it could do with some work. Could do with a lick of paint, too. But it's warm and it's home. I've lived in worse places."

Jay chuckled as he moved to collect sugar and creamer. "I hear you. I've lived in some absolute hovels over the years, particularly before making it big. It's probably what gave us cast iron immune systems."

Dominic appeared to be lost in taking in his surroundings and Jay was happy that he'd given the other man a chance. He watched as the dark-haired man reached down to pick up Blue, carefully draping the cat over one shoulder and petting his back. The tiny gesture of acceptance warmed Jay and he reached for the creamer in order to hide his smile.

"Yeah, might get around to fixing it up this summer."

"Summer's busy here, too," Jay commented. "I'll give you a hand if you need it."

Normally he would have kicked himself for offering but the look of joy on Dominic's face was too adorable to resist.

"That would be great! Thanks!"

Jay grinned and poured coffee into the waiting mugs. "You're welcome. Cream? Sugar?"

With the mugs in his hands, Jay lead the little procession of Dominic and Blue back into the living area. His ass hadn't hit the seat before he was roused by the scrapping of a chair on the stone floor. Looking up, he found Dominic pushing the other chair from the opposite side of the fire. Blue, little attention seeker that he was, had already taken up residence in the spot that Dominic's ass would soon occupy.

"I don't want to sit across the room from you," Dominic explained with a smile. "Sorry. Feels impersonal."

Jay shrugged. "That's okay. We could have sat on the couch." He nodded to the sagging, yet comfortable, three-seat couch that sat just beyond where Dominic's chair had been. "Just don't sit on the cat."

Dominic's smile was still sparkling in all its glory as he scooped the cat up and sat himself down. He stretched his legs out and put the cat in his lap. Once relaxed Dominic seemed to ooze sexuality and Jay sipped at his coffee to distract himself.

"So what about you, Dominic? Wife? Girlfriend?"

The dark-haired man shook his head and gazed at the fire, his free hand resting on Blue's back. "No. Not since I moved out here. Like you said, it's a transient town. People are here for either of the tourist seasons and only want a quick fling. I'm too old for that."

"I get that. It gets harder the older you get, too."

Dominic snorted and strands of hair fell into his eyes. "Doesn't it just? Guys see an older guy and think Sugar Daddy. I need a Sugar Son, someone who's gonna help keep the lights on."

Jay's attention was piqued. Had Dominic just admitted to being gay? Not that he himself was looking for anyone but he still decided to press a little further.

"What was your last partner like?"

With his eyes on the fire, Dominic appeared to drift off into a land of memories. There was a gentle smile on his lips. "Bit younger than me. Blonde hair. Worked in a bar. Came and worked a few seasons for me prepping food and helping serve at events. He moved to Vegas because there's more money in bar-tending there especially for someone good looking."

Jay slouched down into his chair and kept his

attention on Dominic. The other man had disappeared into a completely different realm and whether he felt comfortable or not, Jay didn't know. What he did know was that Dominic had outed himself, whether he'd meant to or not.

"So what do you look for in a partner?" he finally asked.

Dominic's shoulders rose and fell. "Once upon a time, young and fast. These days? Someone stable. Someone who's not gonna fuck around on me. Someone who's done their lost weekends."

Someone like me, Jay thought. *But do I really want to get into a relationship with this guy? Is he what I'm looking for? Or have I just become desperate because I'm cooped up in a small cottage in a tiny mountain town with very few options?*

Silence fell over them. For once it wasn't one of the awkward silences that Jay had grown so used to. The silence when he came out to his therapist. The silence when he came out to his wife. The silence when eventually returned home and found a house that was devoid of anything that belonged to him. They'd been strained, heavy silences that had occasionally been punctuated by sobbing, screaming, and the shattering of crockery. There had been so much pain that Jay hadn't been sure how to process it all and the temptation to sit at a bar and drink himself to death had been all too real.

Dominic was the first to break the quiet that hung over them by talking about restaurants in the town. Which lead to Jay asking him about his former barbecuing business. Big D's Barbecue had been a mobile business with Dominic hauling his staff in a huge, silver catering RV with a smoker rattling behind them. His descriptions of a different life on the road made Jay smile and he found himself settling in as Dominic shifted from talking about driving his RV, to cooking all night, to serving thousands of people.

Eventually Dominic looked from Jay and to one of the tiny windows. "As much as I don't wanna move, I better get going. It's snowing again."

Glancing to the window, Jay could indeed see snowflakes swirling through the darkness and around the porch light. He sighed softly and took Dominic's mug from him.

"You gonna be okay out there?" he asked.

"I will if I leave before it gets any heavier. Don't want you to have to put me up for the night," he finished with a grin.

Jay returned the dark-haired man's smile. "Not that I'd care even if I did. Seems normal practice around here."

He felt his heart ache as he watched Dominic stand and gently place the cat back on the chair. Blue looked up at them both with large, almost sad, eyes and Jay silently apologised to him. Dominic paused at the door and, for one heart-stopping moment, Jay though that maybe, just maybe, there would be something a little more.

Instead, Dominic gave him that wide, sunny smile. The soft light of the lamps twinkled in his eyes and his hair had become ruffled from where he'd leaned back in the chair.

"Night, Jay. Thank you for a great evening. I'll see

you later, okay?"

All he could do was nod dumbly until his voice decided to regain residency in his body. "Yeah. It's been great. Thanks for helping me to come out of my shell. Appreciate it."

"You're welcome." Dominic swept away a handful of hair that had fallen over his eyes and looked out into the cold darkness. "Well, I'll catch you later. Come by the shop if you want more coffee and conversation."

And, with that, Dominic was gone. Jay leaned against the door frame and sighed as he watched the other man get into his car. Dominic gave him a wave before backing out onto the road and disappearing into the darkness.

Chapter 5

Sunlight streamed through the round windows and Jay found himself staring at the white ceiling. His brain was whirling with the memories of the previous evening. He didn't want to admit it to himself but he'd had fun. And, deep down, there was something swirling deep inside of him. Warm, happy, fluttering, it danced around his stomach and up to his heart.

He'd got up, fed Blue, and gone back to bed to mull everything over. Jay knew that he had to admit up to certain things, mostly that he'd had fun the previous evening and that he was also feeling something for Dominic. No one had come into his life in recent years and just wanted to sit and talk to him. Most people were fans looking for something they could use to further their own lives. Or they were promoters, or therapists, or someone else connected with his business. No one just wanted to sit and... talk.

Except for Dominic.

And no matter how hard he tried, Jay couldn't shake the feelings that lingered in his soul.

Dragging himself from the bed, Jay showered and dressed. He couldn't listen to the voices in his head any longer. He had to get out and do something.

Not bothering with breakfast, Jay just shoved himself out of the door and began the walk into Waybridge. Starting at the top of Main Street, he grabbed a couple of take-out coffees from Joe's and made his way down to Dominic's shop.

Stopping outside of his new friend's shop, Jay frowned. He could see a light but, unlike the other shops on the street, the windows were white with frost.

Using his back, he pushed the door open and was instantly hit by a draft of cold air. Jay flinched as he pushed his way inside and tried to ignore the plumes of white that exited his own mouth.

"Jesus, Dominic, it's freezing! Why's your heating not on?"

"No oil," came the mumbled reply.

A figure wrapped in blankets sat hunched behind the counter. A beanie was pulled over their head and their gloved fingers moved pieces of a jigsaw puzzle around the wooden surface.

"But there's oil on the way?" Jay placed a cardboard cup in front of Dominic. "Drink this. It'll warm you up."

Even Dominic's glasses were misted with a thin layer of condensation. The look in his eyes told Jay all that he needed to know. Reaching into his pocket, Jay pulled out his phone.

"Let me call the supplier for you."

"No! Jay, I'll sort it! I just haven't got round to calling them yet."

Dominic's response caused Jay to take a step back. He didn't do well with confrontation and he could already feel himself fighting between crawling back into his shell or letting his rockstar temper take flight.

"Dominic, it's freezing in here. Literally. And the apartment will be cold, too-"

"Tell me about it! I slept through it." Dominic's face twisted with annoyance. "Wish I'd stayed at yours last night."

Breathe. Just breathe. Don't let your temper flare. You're better than that now it's the last thing that either of you need right now.

Deep down, Jay knew that Dominic wasn't going to "sort" the heating. They both knew that Dominic didn't have a cent to his name and that all the money he'd made from the sale of his previous business had gone back into his new one.

Jay's breathing slowed and he stepped back towards the counter. He couldn't let Dominic's reluctance to accept his help get to him. Behind the scenes, his temper was well known. While his drummer had controlled the public aspect of the band, Jay had controlled the artistic output. He was used to getting his own way, even if it meant occasionally flipping out at someone. But flipping out at Dominic wasn't an option. Dominic needed help, not someone screaming in his face and demanding answers.

But he could help in other ways.

"I've got a couple of portable oil radiators at the cottage," Jay said softly. He trod carefully in order to not to crack Dominic's fragile exterior any more than he already had. "You can have those until you get some oil."

Dominic's stony expression softened and he finally took a drink of his coffee. "Thanks. I'll drive you home after I've drunk this and pick 'em up."

Jay chose to remain silent. Instead he gave Dominic a gentle smile and felt the other man relax.

"Gotta keep this place warm somehow," Dominic continued. "Otherwise the sheet music will get damp. Then it'll be ruined and I'll be shit outta luck."

"We'll get you warmed up." Jay clutched his own coffee and felt the warmth seep into his numb fingertips. "Why don't you stay at mine tonight? You can put both radiators down here and save your stock."

The words left his mouth so quickly that Jay didn't have time to process what was actually going on. Regret instantly clenched at him and he quickly reminded himself that life was different now. He didn't have to spend his time living in a cocoon. Guests were welcome into his house, even if it would mean that he had to sleep on the couch.

Dominic's shoulders slumped and his face was lit with a warm smile. "That'd be good. Thanks. I'll come by later. Maybe bring some snacks."

"You don't have to bring anything, Dominic. Just yourself."

Having coffee together was becoming a habit that Jay could get used to. Despite the cold, they chatted back and forth, the harsh words of the previous moments melting away with their laughter. When they were finished, Jay tossed the cups into to the trash, bundled Dominic into his car, and made the short trip back to Christmas Cottage.

❄❄❄

Once the small radiators were in Dominic's car, Jay set to work. He kept an eye on the window and waited until Dominic was completely out on the road before grabbing his phone. Scrolling through his contacts, Jay found the number for their PR manager. There was an obvious tone of surprise in her voice when she answered.

"Jay. Didn't think I'd hear from you so soon."

Jay paused his worried pacing and looked out of the window. The view beyond it was a stunning vista of trees and distant mountains. "Hey, Clara. Can you not tell anyone that I called."

"Sure. What can I do for you?"

He went on to explain about Dominic and his store and how the other man was struggling financially. "He won't accept my help," Jay concluded. "But he doesn't have to know that I drummed up some PR for him. Can you do it?"

"It'll cost you, Jay."

"You know where to get the money."

"I do," she replied. "I'll start small so it doesn't look obvious. Get the local media involved. I'm looking at his social media now and it looks like the quirky kind of place that influencers love so I'll send some of them along."

Jay cringed at the mere mention of social media but mumbled an agreement all the same. He didn't know how Dominic would feel with people posing next to, or with, his prized stock but it was a risk that, for the moment, they'd have to take.

"Then we'll work our way up," Clara continued. "The *New Yorker,* the *LA Times* etc. Maybe some of the resort publications. Next time you go in, see if you can find some of your own music in there and send over a photo. I'll get it up on the band's page to give him a quick boost of customers. Don't worry; I won't reveal that it's your home, nor that you took the

54

photo."

She paused and Jay heard her sip at her ever present cup of coffee before gently asking, "You really like this guy, huh?"

Jay nodded to himself. "I do. Didn't think I would and tried to fight off the feelings. But I do like him."

"Don't fight it, Jay. When you're ready, tell him how you feel. I think you're going to be pleasantly surprised. I've got a hunch that he likes you, too."

Pulling himself onto the window ledge, Jay allowed himself to melt against the brickwork. A small smile, the latest in a long line of smiles, tickled his lips. "Thanks."

"You're welcome." He could hear hear the smile in her voice. "Anything else I can do for you, Jay?"

"Not at the minute. Thanks for doing this, Clara. I really appreciate it."

"No worries. And don't be a stranger, okay? Everyone misses you."

"I won't," he quietly replied. "At least not forever."

Chapter 6

The temperatures were dropping and night was slowly easing its way in. Pink and orange melted across the sky with hints of cloud add a little shadow to the aerial display.

Jay had pondered how Dominic was doing and whether he'd managed to sufficiently warm the shop. He hoped that the other man was managing to keep warm enough until it was time for him to land at Christmas Cottage.

A stew was bubbling away in a crock pot with its rich, meaty smell hanging over the kitchen. Potatoes bubbled in a pan on the hob and Jay laid the table for the first time since moving in. It was rare that he sat there. Mostly he used the table for dumping dirty dishes before he took them through to the kitchen. Normally he ate standing in the kitchen or seated in front of the fire. As had become habit, he ate with his plate held above his head as an already-fed Blue howled for more.

"Should have called you Oliver," was Jay's mealtime mantra.

There was soda chilling in the fridge and Blue sat at his feet to snaffle any pieces of beef that "accidentally" fell on the floor. The hurricane lamps had been moved to the far end of the table. Jay rarely used the larger room's overhead lights, preferring a softer, more natural, light to what the electric powered ones provided.

Through the narrow kitchen doorway, Jay saw headlights swing up to the house. Wiping his hands on a towel, he nudged Blue out of the way and walked to the door. He opened it just in time to find Dominic heaving a bag from the back seat of his car.

"Need a hand?"

Dominic straightened up and swung the bag onto his shoulder. "I'm fine." He stooped to reach back into the car and pulled out a paper bag from the supermarket. "Just needed this."

Leaning against the door frame, Jay said, "I said that you didn't need to bring anything other than yourself."

"Snacks. For if, you know, we get talking late into the night." Dominic shrugged as he walked up to the house.

Jay took in Dominic's pale complexion and the dark rings beneath his eyes. "The only thing you'll be doing tonight is eating and getting some sleep." He moved aside to let the other man in. "Come on in, Dominic. There's food cooking and I'm sure your fuzzy friend would be happy to see you."

Dominic hadn't so much as stepped through the door before Blue was winding around his ankles.

Reaching down, Jay swept the large cat into his arms. "Let the man in, please."

He watched as Dominic dropped his bags and closed the door. There appeared to be a small smile on Dominic's lips. The constant happiness and amusement was something that Jay liked about him. There seemed to be a perpetual twinkle in Dominic's eyes and life appeared to not bother him as much as it did other people.

Once Dominic was settled, Jay returned to the

kitchen. He ladled stew and potatoes into two large bowls and took it to the table. Blue had already made himself at home in Dominic's arms with his little grey head tucked beneath the dark-haired man's chin.

"He certainly likes you." Jay places the bowls on the table. "Soda? Water? I haven't got alcohol in the house. Sorry."

"Soda's fine. Thanks." Dominic gave the cat a kiss before carefully placing him on a chair beside the fire. "Do you need any help?"

Pausing at the kitchen entrance, Jay looked to the other man and shook his head. "I'm good, thanks. You make yourself at home."

He returned to the kitchen and grabbed a couple of sodas from the fridge. Jay could feel the butterflies taking flight in his stomach. He knew that he had to listen to Clara and take her advice. *Don't try and push it away. Let it happen.*

But what if he didn't want it to happen? What if he was happy alone?

Even Jay had to admit that he wasn't happy and that the loneliness was creeping in and eating away at his soul. With a sigh, he turned from the kitchen and stepped out back into the living area.

"Blue, no!" Jay sighed and placed the two cans on the table before fully taking in the sight before him.

Dominic was standing and had both bowls held high above his head. The cat, little menace to society that he was, was dancing on the table. Picking the cat up, Jay gave him a quick kiss and put him on the floor.

"You've been fed. Please let us eat in peace."

Jay didn't want to believe that animals could understand them. But Blue gave him such a look of disgust that Jay felt his own soul freeze. The cat huffed and hopped up onto a chair.

"Sorry about that." Reaching out, he took the bowls from Dominic and returned them to the table. "Please eat before it gets cold, or the cat gets it."

Seating himself at the table, Jay took in the room. He'd never really sat at the table for long periods of time and so the perspective was one that was completely new to him. The fire warmed his back and the chandelier's branches curled above his head. Shadows cast by the lamps on the table weaved among the rafters. Jay felt a shiver dance down his spine and he settled into his chair with a small smile on his lips.

"Happy?" he heard Dominic ask.

"Huh? Yeah. I suppose I am. Just admiring the ceiling." Jay looked up again. "I've never sat at the table so I'm seeing the house from a new angle here. Really glad I bought it. I'm kind of looking forward to hunkering down in here during monsoon season. Or maybe add a shelter to the back of the house so that we can sit out there."

So that we can sit out there? What are you doing, Hammond?

He saw Dominic's eyebrows momentarily flick up but the other man said nothing other than, "Sounds perfect. You like the rain?"

"I like nature," Jay softly replied. "I like everything that comes with it. It gives me the peace and serenity that I couldn't always find in my other life."

59

"So why'd you become a musician?" For someone who'd shovelled his previous meal into his mouth, Dominic was suddenly taking his time. "Seems odd for someone who wants a solitary life."

Resting the spoon on the edge of the bowl, Jay leaned back into his chair and once more stared at the ceiling above himself. "You know, I probably can't give you a more detailed answer than I love music. Always have done. It was an escape from an otherwise imperfect life. I enjoyed playing guitar and singing. We tried to find another singer for the band but that never worked out. Eventually I was able to overcome enough of the anxiety to be the person you saw on stage. Off stage..."

"You're a completely different person?"

Jay took a deep breath and allowed a smile to paint itself onto his lips. He looked back to Dominic and nodded. "Exactly. I'm the quiet guy who enjoys being by himself or with a select handful of people. I enjoy being away from it all, breathing in clear air, and sitting beside creeks. You get the idea."

"Sounds like heaven," Dominic murmured before having another mouthful of food. "This stew is amazing, by the way."

A blush touched his cheeks and Jay lowered his head. "Thanks."

They ate in silence for a while and Jay basked in the homeliness of having company and a good meal. But something from their previous evening together was still bugging him.

"Dominic," he quietly began, "you mentioned something about a problem with alcohol. Mind if I ask you about that?"

Across the table, Dominic paused before sighing. He held the spoon for a moment before lowering it back into the bowl. Jay could sense a cloud settling over the other man and he kicked himself for even asking the question.

"Truth be told, it's a few things," Dominic replied. "Like I said at the restaurant, the weather's been getting to me. On top of that, you know that I'm broke. The store has zero money. I have zero money. This is the first real meal I've eaten in a couple of days. Most of the time I live on noodles and bread. That trip to the coffee shop, the night that we met, that was my little treat to myself for making a sale that day. I'd sold some books so decided to have a coffee and see some people. The snacks I bought tonight; I used the money from your sale to get those." Dominic lifted his head and brushed the hair from his eyes. Jay could see the sorrow in his face. He'd wanted a new start. Wanted to reinvent himself. Yet, unlike his other projects, this one looked as though it was failing.

"I can give you money-"

Dominic sadly laughed and shook his head. "I don't want your money. What you're doing right now, right here, is enough. You've shown kindness and friendship when you didn't have to. You've admitted that you're not keen on having people around, especially in your house. Yet you've opened yours up for me."

Dominic's voice was cracking and Jay could see tears beginning to swim through his eyes. The other man heaved a handful of hair back of his shoulder and took a deep, shuddering breath. "I'm sorry."

"Don't be sorry," Jay replied. "You have nothing to be sorry for. But, please, let me know if you need anything. I know you've got those radiators now but I'll happily get the tanks filled until business starts picking up for you. And let me put some food in your fridge. Or come and eat here. Dominic, I love my solitude. But company is also nice. And, well, Blue seems to have taken to you."

There was a soft *meow* from the chair behind him and Jay smiled. "See? He likes having you here."

And I do, too. I'm finally going to admit to liking your company.

Dominic's sadness faded a little. "Thanks, I appreciate it. And I know I was being stubborn but I'd really appreciate a little help. But just a little, okay?"

His heart warmed at Dominic's replied and Jay allowed himself to relax a little more. "Thank you. And you're welcome."

The silence fell over them again. Not even Blue was pestering for food. *It's like he knows,* Jay thought.

It was Dominic who finally spoke, his spoon chiming against his now-empty bowl as he pushed everything to one side. "Where do you want me to sleep? I can take the couch."

Jay shook his head and continued to mop at the last of the gravy with a hunk of bread. "Sleep in the bed. You need a good night. I'll take the couch. Not the first time I've fallen asleep there," he finished with a chuckle.

"I don't want to impose on you."

Dominic's voice was so soft and so gentle that Jay

felt like crying. There seemed to be two Dominics; the outgoing one who lived at the shop and the quieter, gentler one that lived in the shadows.

Again, Jay shook his head. "You're not imposing. I promise. Sleep in the bed and you'll feel much better in the morning. I promise."

Chapter 7

The fire had died down to a dull glow. Dominic, and Blue, had long since made their way up to bed. Jay had tried reading by the light of the fire and then, as that had faded, by the light of his cell phone. But he'd found the strain on his eyes too much. Instead, he lay on his back and looked up at the darkness that arched away above him.

The couch wasn't as comfortable as he'd made it out to be. He had fallen asleep on it several times before but he'd always woken with a crick in his neck and an ache in his lower back. Admitting that he wasn't eighteen any more had been hard on Jay and falling asleep on a couch only reaffirmed that. But, as he kept reminding himself, it was only for a few nights until they got Dominic's heating tanks refilled.

"Jay?"

Dominic's lilting voice caused him to start and Jay let out an involuntary groan as his legs untangled themselves from the opposite end of the couch. Grabbing his phone, Jay flicked on the flashlight and aimed it in the direction of Dominic's voice.

"Jesus, Dominic! I didn't hear you come down." He paused to catch his breath. "Sorry. I'm sorry. You okay?"

Dominic stood beside the couch with a wicked case of bedhead and the darkest doe-eyes Jay had ever seen. He felt himself falling a little deeper, his heart aching a little more as he looked over the other man's flannel pyjamas.

"Come to bed, Jay? I can hear you tossing and

turning and quietly cursing to yourself. Plus your cat's wondering where you are."

Heat rose to Jay's cheeks and he struggled to sit upright. "But where will you sleep?"

"Up there. With you. Don't worry. I'll stay on my side of the bed."

"I- Dominic, I don't know." Thrown by what Dominic had said, Jay raked his hands through his hair and glanced to the couch. It really wasn't comfortable and he could already feel the ache in his back. By morning it would be a roaring ball of pain nestled in the small on his back.

"It'll be fine. I promise," Dominic gently said.

But would it? Jay could already feel another ache growing, this one in his stomach. And he knew that, before long, it would work its way down into his groin. Chewing on his lower lip, he looked away from Dominic and quickly debated everything. Sleeping in his bed would be good. He'd definitely be more comfortable. But he'd be sharing that space with the finest of temptations. Jay was sure he'd be able to keep his hands to himself. But what about Dominic? Could he be trusted to do the same?

Sighing, Jay got to his feet. "You're right. I can't sleep down here. And what's gonna happen, right?"

Dominic nodded in the low light and Jay could just make out the barest whisper of a smile on his lips. "Exactly. Come on. Your cat's waiting for you."

They walked through the house in silence, the stairs creaking beneath their feet. Only the beside lamp was on, its light warm and welcoming. Blue was curled at the end of the bed and quietly *chirruped* when he saw his owner. Smiling, Jay gave the cat a head scratch before sitting on the edge of the bed. His heart was in his throat and he could hear the blood pounding through his ears. The last time he'd shared a bed with a man had been thirty or more years ago. And that was only because there had been a lack of places to sleep. Young bands made do with whatever they had, even if it meant two or three of them huddling in a single bed.

Stretching himself out, Jay tucked his feet beneath the covers. He felt the bed depress and looked up to see Dominic doing the same. The dark-haired man gave him a small smile before brushing his hair over his shoulders.

"Sleep well, Jay."

He shuffled up the bed until his shoulders rested against the pillows. "Yeah. You, too."

The light turned out with a click and darkness finally swamped the house. Bar Dominic's breathing and Blue's not-so-subtle snoring, the house was silent. Almost painfully silent.

Jay tried to get comfortable without disturbing his bedfellows. He twisted his hips until he was lying on his side and tucked his hands beneath the pillows. He closed his eyes and tried to focus on nothing but the darkness. But all he could think of was the weight of the person across the bed. No one else had slept in the bed with him. No one else had graced the sheets or left their scent behind. And Dominic had become very comfortable very quickly.

"Jay?"

"Yeah?"

"Are you okay?"

Rolling onto his back, Jay sighed and tucked his hands beneath his head. "Yeah-" He paused and swallowed around the lump in his throat. It was time to admit everything. "No. No, I'm not."

The bed shifted once more and he watched Dominic's shadowy form sit up. "I'll go sleep on the couch."

Reaching out, he grabbed at Dominic's shoulder. "No. Don't do that. That's not what I mean." Jay could feel everything welling up. Every emotion was thundering through him, all of them fighting for his attention. "Dominic, I want you here. In bed. With me."

There. He'd said it. And there was nothing more to say.

The air between them seemed to thicken with tension and Jay felt his heart go into free fall. He thought that Dominic felt the same, yet he'd obviously read the other man wrong.

Dominic's voice was quiet and gentle. "You want me to stay here?"

"Yeah," he murmured. "Here. With me."

Please don't make me beg, Dominic. Please don't force me to open up any more. Not just yet anyway.

He saw Dominic's shadowy figure shrug before he heaved himself back into bed. There was a wave of warm breath as Dominic faced him and Jay allowed himself to relax a little.

"Hey," Dominic whispered.

"Hey." Jay could feel his throat tightening and tears stinging his eyes.

"Wanna tell me what's on your mind?"

"In the morning. Please?"

Jay could have cried over Dominic's gentleness. The other man seemed to have a genuine interest in what was happening. And, even though he was asking pressing questions, he wasn't forcing Jay to answer.

The blankets moved in what Jay translated as a shrug before Dominic asked, "Anything I can do to help you?"

Stay here. Don't move. Don't leave. Keep me warm. Maybe, just maybe, love me...

But how to say those things? How to even convey them? Stricken with the fear that he now had to do something, Jay had no clue how to even speak.

Instead, he reached out and placed a gentle finger against Dominic's cheek. He stroked in the same manner as he did with the cat, his finger finding the smooth swell of a cheek before grazing against the rough stubble of Dominic's beard. A soft sigh tickled his own face and he felt Dominic relax into the bed.

"Feels good, Jay," Dominic whispered.

"Yeah?"

"Yeah. You don't have to stop."

Jay smiled at those five words and allowed his hand to flatten and cup Dominic's chin. Beneath his fingers the other man shivered and shifted a little closer. The tension had faded and the air held a more delicious energy. Leaning closer, Jay touched his lips to Dominic's cheek and savoured the feeling of the other man's skin against his own. Everything stilled around him; for so long he'd wanted to be with another man. For so long he'd dreamed about having them close. For so long he'd dreamed of what it would feel like. And now it was happening, and in his own bed no less.

Dominic shifted once more and Jay felt lips as soft as satin brush against his own. He caught his breath and his hand stilled against Dominic's jaw, his thumb pressed against the other man's beard.

"Hey," Dominic quietly said. "This okay?"

Jay was silent for a moment before sliding his hand from Dominic's cheek and into the crook of his neck. Those waves of hair spilled over his fingers and Jay ached for the moment that he could finally touch it properly.

Not wanting to break the spell that hung over them, he gently replied, "This is perfectly okay."

Dominic smiled against his mouth and a hand came to rest in his own back. "Good."

All that existed was their warm cocoon of the bed. Hidden away from the cold world outside, they could do anything they wanted. And Jay highly intended on doing so. He wanted his inhibitions to crumble away and leave him free to live the life that he'd always dreamed of. Spending the vast majority of his life behind the doors of his proverbial closet. Lack of living was what had caused so many sleeplessness nights.

Jay allowed himself to melt into the bed as the kiss deepened. Dominic seemed like an easy going guy and probably wouldn't care what did, or didn't, happen. He'd just chalk it up to having fun. Even with that in mind, Jay didn't want to give too much away and risk having his already-fragile heart being shattered.

With Dominic's lips pressed against his own, Jay felt as though he was flying. His head was swimming and his heart pounded. And, despite every reservation that he still held, he didn't want the moment to end. He wanted to wrap himself around Dominic and never let the other man up. He wanted to taste every delight that Dominic had to offer. He wanted to learn, and to teach, and to grow and finally become the man that he'd always wanted to be.

It seemed that someone else didn't want the moment to end as Dominic rolled his hips with a guttural groan. "So good. You feel so fuckin' good."

Jay smiled against the other man's lips. Dominic wasn't the only one who was feeling good. By the bulge in his own pyjama pants, Jay could conclude that it was a mutual feeling.

"Want more?" Dominic asked.

The only response that Jay could give was a deep groan. His hips moved against Dominic's and he didn't falter as the other man wrapped a leg around him. The moved as one, the bed creaking quietly as they each pushed against the other. It felt far better than Jay had ever imagined it would. He felt elated, and dizzy, and a strange sense of sickness, the kind that struck as something new entered your life. Warm, sticky pre-come dampened the front of his thin pyjama pants and Jay could feel the knot in his stomach tightening. Dominic was wound around him, his hands stroking along Jay's back and his leg pulling Jay closer. There was little that Jay could do other than go along with the ride and enjoy every moment of it.

His own fingers gently squeezed the back of Dominic's neck as he pulled the other man a little closer. Parting his lips, Jay darted his tongue over Dominic's lips. That was all it took for Dominic to open up and their sighs became a little louder and their rocking became a little harder. The headboard tapped against the wall and, yet, Jay didn't have a care in the world. Dominic's fingers slid in his hair, first smoothing the curls at the nap of his neck, before pulling him closer and deepening the kiss. Teeth nipped at Jay's lower lip before backing away to replace the pain with the gentlest of touches.

With his head swimming, Jay pulled back and rested his head against Dominic's. The other man's name whispered past his lips as the knot in his groin became painfully tight. Everything was hazy and the world had faded to nothing but the point of pleasure. He could hear himself growing a little louder, his voice becoming a little deeper. The bedsheets were balled into his free hand as his hips continued to move against Dominic. Warm breath washed over his ears as Dominic whispered to him, encouraged him, and pushed him closer to that final release.

And finally everything broke. The pleasure snapped through him like a lightning bolt. Shards of light burst behind his eyes and Jay heard his voice let out a strangled moan. Riding out the waves of his orgasm was almost painful and he willed them to soften and allow him to enjoy the moment.

So long. It's been so long since I've felt like this.
The life he'd once known, the one he'd lived for

nearly sixty years, was crumbling away. Confined to history, that life was finally no more. Yet the panic still lingered in his soul. The morals that had been instilled in him were still there, whispering idle threats to him.

It's my time. My time to live. You're no longer relevant. It's time for you to leave.

"Jay?" Dominic's voice, while soft, sounded distant. "Jay?"

Opening his eyes, Jay gave Dominic a soft smile. "Hey."

"Hi. Thought I'd lost you there. How you feelin'?"

His eyes felt heavy and slid closed as he nodded. "Good. Feelin' good. You?"

"Same." Dominic's hand cupped the back of his head.

Pushing a hand beneath the covers, Jay shuffled his now-soiled pants off and kicked them out the bed. "Need a change?" he asked.

He felt Dominic shake his head. "I'm good. I'll sleep naked. Hope you don't mind."

A grin tugged at Jay's lips. "Considering what just happened, not in the slightest."

Dominic's hand slid from his neck and over his shoulders. There was comfort in having another touch him so tenderly. Jay allowed himself to relax as he pulled Dominic closer. Things were changing and, for once, they seemed to be changing for the better.

Chapter 8

For the first time in a long time, Jay woke with a smile on his face. Opening his eyes in the early morning light, he was overjoyed to find Dominic still sleeping beside him, his hands tucked beneath him and his dark hair cascading over the pillows. Blue was curled up by the headboard, his purring becoming louder as he caught Jay waking.

He reached out and scratched Blue's head. "Morning. Shall we go and make some breakfast?"

Doing his best not to wake Dominic, Jay slid from the bed and made his way downstairs. As with every morning, Blue insisted on racing him to the kitchen and sitting beside his bowl. The smile that Jay wore wasn't just for his cat's antics; it was for the sense of peace that was beginning to settle in his soul. The feeling that everything was going to be okay.

Once he'd fed the cat, Jay got down to making breakfast. Normally he ate toast and drank coffee while looking out of the window. But, for the first time ever, he had a guest in his house. So he settled on pancakes and bacon to get Dominic started with what would no doubt be a busy day full of people passing by the shop.

He was just preparing to pour batter into the pan when he felt something rest against his shoulder. Warm breath kissed his cheek and an arm rested at his waist. Jay smiled gently and lifted his head to look at Dominic.

The other man was still lethargic and his long hair was an almost adorable mess. His dark eyes, still glazed with sleep, gazed up at Jay.

"Morning. Sleep well?"

Dominic nodded against his shoulder. "Um-hm."

"Would you like some breakfast before going and checking on the shop?"

"Um-hm."

"Not a morning person?"

Dominic shook his head. "Uh-uh."

Putting the spatula to one side, Jay reached up and stroked the other man's head. "Go and make yourself comfortable and I'll bring you a plate and some coffee."

Jay smiled as Dominic walked away. Smiling; he seemed to be doing a lot more of that, and he couldn't help himself. Dominic, Jay was glad to say, was making him happy. Happier than he'd been in a long time. And, for the first time, he thought nothing of his new life. The crushing thoughts of morals and ethics and the life that he'd previous lead seemed to have vanished with the night. Having Dominic in the house, and in his bed, seemed to be perfectly normal.

The pan sizzled as he added oil and then the batter. It didn't take long before he had a plate of pancakes and a hot mug of coffee ready to go. Stepping over Blue, Jay made his way through to the living area. Dominic was hunched at the table, his hair hanging around his face and his eyes on his hands. He was obviously still tired and not in the mood for being disturbed. Putting the plate and mug in front of the other man, Jay ran a hand over Dominic's head.

"Eat up and get some colour back in that face."

❄❄❄

Once Dominic was fed, showered, and out of the door, Jay took care of himself. Eating breakfast with someone else had been almost reassuring. There had been a warmth in the air and there had been none of strained silence that he'd expected. He'd caught himself glancing at the dark-haired man, taking in the way he ate and occasionally looked around himself. Dominic had been lost in his own early morning world, obviously thinking over what he was going to do with his store.

He showered and dressed before making himself another coffee. Standing at the kitchen window, Jay stared out at the crisp, freshly fallen snow. He truly did love being out in the wilderness. Loved seeing nature at its best.

Blue jumped up and settled himself on the sill, his eyes focused on what little wildlife was foraging in the garden. Jay smiled softly and scratched the cat's head.

"We'll get you a bird feeder in the summer so that you can sit and watch them."

Blue flicked his ears back to listen and quietly *chirruped*.

Jay had enjoyed his morning with Dominic. He'd enjoyed waking up next to someone. Enjoyed making food for them. Enjoyed their company. His earlier reservations about Dominic were slowly melting away. Where once Jay had seen someone who was boisterous and over the top, he now saw someone who may be lonely. Dominic gave off the air that all was right in his world but the revelations of the past day had taught Jay far more about the man from the music shop.

His heart ached at the thought of Dominic freezing and hungry in his shop. He was just about to haul his coat on when his phone vibrated with a message.

First influencers have gone in. Why don't you get down there and get me some photos of your music? Take Blue. People LOVE cats. C xxx PS: So...??

Jay couldn't help but grin at Clara's message.

On my way now. Will put Blue in his little coat. So... We're spending time together.

It took her less than ten seconds to reply.

YES! Jay, he'll be soooo good for you! Go and enjoy your day. ;) xxx

It didn't take much to convince Blue to get into his little red jacket and harness. He enjoyed taking walks out in the snow, often riding on Jay's shoulders and taking in the scents and scenery. Blue was an indoor cat. Always had been. And Jay had no intention of ever letting him go outdoors alone. There were too many animals in the mountains that would happily take the cat for their dinner. So walks, and shoulder rides, it was.

"You're a good boy," Jay murmured as he dressed himself. "Can't believe you're as chill as you are."

Wrapped in a thick coat and walking boots, Jay draped the cat over his shoulder and headed out into the winter wonderland. Tire tracks, evidence of Dominic's earlier departure, cut through the snow and wound down the road. Placing his feet in them, Jay followed the wide tracks off the driveway and down into the town.

The walk down into Waybridge was always pleasant. It was even nicer with a cat wrapped around his neck. The only downside was being stopped every few metres by people wanting to say hi to Blue. Jay felt himself recalling the person that he once was, the person who stood on stage and addressed the crowds. For a while he could hide behind that persona and brighten peoples days as they lined up to fuss his cat. And Blue, ever the people-pleaser, was taking it all in.

Nestled into Jay's neck and purring loudly, Blue was as happy as a clam by the time they reached Between the Sheets.

Yet there were more people who were suddenly interested in meeting the jacketed grey cat. In the handful of times that Jay had entered the shop, he'd never seen it as busy as it was in that moment. One couple were beside the window, creating what Jay believed to be some artful photograph of loose sheet music. Another woman was flicking through books while someone, presumably her boyfriend or photographer, took photographs of her. A man sat before a rack of music, carefully lifting books and taking a photo before putting it back. Jay turned to the register and found a slightly stunned Dominic staring at the room before him.

"All day," the dark-haired man said quietly. "They've been coming in all day and taking photos."

"Anyone bought anything?"

Dominic's eyes snapped to his while the shocked look remained. "Yeah. A couple. Oh, you bought Blue. Hey, Blue!" Dominic leaned over the counter and gave the cat a stroke.

Shoving his hands under his lazy cat, Jay hoisted him up and gave him to Dominic. "Here. You have him for a minute. I've got to look for something."

He didn't give Dominic another thought as he walked amid the shelves and racks. Everything was sorted alphabetically rather than by genre meaning there was less room for picky customers to argue. Going straight to *W,* Jay flicked through until he found what he was looking for. A smile crossed his lips as he pulled out the sheet music books for *At the End of the World* and *Our Last Stand.* The couple at the window were lingering for a little longer and Jay watched as they took another handful of photographs before tidying away the scene that they'd created. He waited until they were gone before putting the books on the stripped-wood sill. Returning to the counter, he plucked Blue from Dominic's arms and gave the still-shocked man a soft smile.

"Why don't you make us a coffee? I can watch the shop."

"Jay..." Dominic ran a hand through his hair before pushing his glasses back up his nose. "I'm not sure what's going on."

His heart lodged in his throat. Dominic knew something was going on and he wasn't sure whether to tell him or lie. Truth and honesty were the best policy and Jay gave a small nod.

"Go and make coffee and then I'll tell you what's

happening."

With Dominic preoccupied, Jay carried his cat back to the window. Blue, thankfully the most placid cat in the world, was all too happy when Jay lay him beside the books and artfully arranged him. Knowing that he didn't have much time, Jay grabbed his phone from his pocket, moved himself so that he wasn't shooting into the sun and snapped a couple of quick photos of the scene before him. His own music, his cat, and the beautiful mountains in the background made for a wonderful image. With a nod, Jay pocketed his phone and put the books away before retrieving Blue.

"So..." Dominic's voice drifted from the opposite end of the shop. "Can you please tell me what's going on?"

Placing Blue on the counter, Jay took a mug from Dominic and sighed. The other photographers had left but Jay suspected that Clara had more lined up.

"I'm gonna tell you the truth, Dominic. There's no point lying to you and I'm so sorry that I went behind your back." The heat was racing to his cheeks again and Jay swept a curl of hair from his face as he lowered his head. But he couldn't look away. He needed to look Dominic in the eye and he forced himself to raise his head. "Have you looked at your social media today?"

Dominic shook his head. His voice was low and almost scared as he replied, "No. No, I haven't."

"I called our PR manager and told her what was happening with you and the store. She's getting you some attention. The people that have been coming in all day are influencers. They'll be posting about the store on social media. Soon, maybe after Christmas, there'll be physical media – magazines, newspapers, and the like – coming in. I want to help you, Dominic, really I do. You wouldn't take my money so I'm hoping and praying that you'll take everything else that I have to offer." Jay could feel tears beginning to prickle his eyes and he realised that he hadn't felt so scared since he'd confessed to being gay. The thought of losing Dominic was tearing him apart and he furiously fought back the agony that screamed through him. "Dominic, I like you. I like you a lot. And all I want to do is help."

The other man was looking at him in stunned silence. Jay was convinced Dominic was going to lose his temper just as he had done a handful of days earlier. Taking a deep breath, Jay took a step back and waited.

"You did what?" Dominic finally asked.

"I asked our PR manager to turn some attention on you. She's hardly busy at the minute and she likes doing what she does." He deliberately omitted "help people" because he really didn't want Dominic jumping down his throat.

"How much does she know about me?"

Again, Jay measured his words. "That your stock would be ruined because of a fault in your heating."

"So you didn't tell her I was broke?"

"Would it have made a difference if I did?"

Dominic shrugged and glanced down at the mug in his hands. "I suppose not."

A silence fell over them and, feeling the need to leave, Jay drained his coffee. Dust flitted through the shop's warm, hazy light and Jay felt the homeliness sap away as he prepared to step out into the cold winter day.

"Well." He swallowed around the lump in his throat. "I'll leave you be. There's gonna be other people coming by and you'll soon be back on your feet." He gave Dominic a tight smile.

Dominic just stood and stared at him as though he was a being from another planet. Or had two heads. Or had just done the unthinkable and ruined the best thing that had ever happened to either of them.

Jay nodded and made to pick up Blue. He felt a movement, a sweep of air, and then hands were clasping his face and lifting it up. Fingers wrapped around the back of his head and tangled in his hair. Lips crushed against his own in a desperate, heated kiss.

And Jay felt the world become still once more.

Chapter 9

Warm light danced from the lamps, creating ever changing pools of light and shadow. The fire crackled and Jay could feel his eyes growing heavy.

An eventful day had ended with a pile of food from Waybridge's single Mexican restaurant. Dominic, it seemed, was a fan of tacos and had turned up on the doorstep with bags of food slung over his arms. Always up for any kind of eating, Jay had joined him at the table as they'd talked over what had happened in the hours since his confession.

"Checked your social media yet?"

Dominic was leaning into the couch with his eyes closed as he soaked up the warmth of the fire. His hands rested on his full stomach and the cat was curled up beside him.

"Um-hm. Checked it while I was at Casa Mexico. It's gone wild, man." Dominic chuckled softly before cracking an eye open. "Thanks, I appreciate it."

Jay smiled. "You didn't have to bring food. I mean, it's not like I have anything else to do with my day other than cook."

"Like I said, it's a thank you for what you've done. My shop was jumping today. So many people coming in and hopefully it'll be even busier tomorrow."

"You're very welcome."

Silence fell over them and Jay allowed himself to drift a little. Everything felt homely, safe even. There was a roaring fire, lamps, a cat purring beside him and a man curled up on the couch. For him, life didn't get more perfect than that.

"What made you decide on a shop?" he finally asked. "You had a catering company, right? What made you to change?"

Dominic shifted beside him, rolling his head on the couch's plump cushions so that he could look Jay in the eye. "Just wanted a change. I don't like being tied down. I like change. I like fucking with the system. Like changing peoples expectations of me."

Jay felt his heart plummet and he glanced down to his knotted hands. "Oh."

"What?"

He sighed and shook his head. "Sorry. Old insecurities. You said you don't like being tied down..."

"I don't like being tied down to *work*." There was a hint of a smile in Dominic's voice. "Doesn't mean I don't want to be tied down to a person. Don't stress yourself, Hammond. You can cook. It's gonna take a lot to get rid of me when I know there's fresh food on the table every day of the week."

Dominic's words were enough to soften him a little. But the little knot of worry still sat in his chest waiting, once more, to burst forth.

"But the barbecue company was rad," Dominic continued. "I loved it. Loved travelling with it. Loved cooking and meeting new people. Took it all over the country and even got invites to go and cook abroad. There was something primal about towing a smoker around, you know? Being on the open road and seeing the night sky from the back of our wagon. Had a huge wagon, too. For food prep and sleeping in. Selling that company was tough but I had to do it. You know that story. I wanted out of the city and somewhere a little more sedate. Kinda feel like I'm getting old here. Everything's so slow. But it's a good slow, right? I mean, yeah, it gets busy. But it's a chilled busy." Dominic paused and sighed. "And I'm rambling, aren't I?"

Grinning, Jay shook his head and took in the way that the fire danced the lenses of Dominic's glasses. "You're not rambling. You've just done a lot of living, Dominic."

"So did you. Damn sight more than I did." There was still a Virginian twang to Dominic's voice that Jay found both endearing and erotic. Years of being on stage and talking to people from around the world had given him what he believed to be a fairly boring voice. His singing was crisp and his speech had a touch of something. But Jay couldn't tell which accent it was that still lingered in his voice.

"Yeah." It was Jay turn to sigh and he looked to the fire. Getting to his feet, he plucked a log from the basket and tossed it to the hungry flames. The wood popped and spluttered before the flames roared up the chimney. "Wasn't all good though. Alcohol and sex addictions. A shitty family situation. Trying to rebuild that family. And, ultimately, having to look real deep inside myself."

"You might have been through a lot of shit in your life. And I mean, *a lot*. But you've done a great job. Jay, you've inspired so many people to look at their own lives and make better decisions. You've been so vocal about it that it's caused people to stop and question their own decisions. You've created a shit ton of music from what's lived in you. And I know your life isn't all roses. They say money doesn't buy happiness. And I know it doesn't. But look at yourself."

Jay could feel the tears beginning to scrape at his eyes. He watched the fire with his hands stuffed in his pockets. Swallowing, Jay tried to fight down his emotions. "I look at myself every day, Dominic. And I hate what I see. Vastly overweight. Hair that desperately needs cutting. *Grey* hair, for fuck's sake. Clothes that hide everything."

Silence. If the door had slammed, he'd have known that Dominic had walked. But he could still feel the other man behind sitting on the couch with his dark eyes boring in to the spot between Jay's shoulders.

"Do you want to know what I see?" Dominic finally asked.

Jay shook his head and raked a hand through the hair that he hated.

"Tough. 'cause I'm gonna fucking tell you. Firstly, I don't give a shit who you are. I don't give a shit about the money that you have or the life that you've lived. What I give a shit about is the man that you are. And it's not all about looks. But if we're going to go that way, *damn*. I see you and I see those eyes that constantly sparkle with innocence and mischief. I see a smile that no one could fake. You know how many people fake a smile these days? Most of them. Not you. Your smile takes over your whole face and that's a fuckin' delight, Jay. It means you're real. You're not bullshitting anyone. You are who you are and you're damn proud of that person even when you feel like you're not. As for your body? Damn, man, I could play with that body all night long. I don't give a flying fuck if you don't like what you look like. I love it. I love the look you've got going. And if you want to lose weight and all of that, I'll fully support you. But that's a decision for you to make. I'm not gonna force it on you."

Jay stood in stunned silence. He didn't want to turn and face Dominic. Didn't want the other man to see the tears that were glazing his eyes. He took a moment for himself before wiping a hand across his eyes and returning to the couch. Settling beside Dominic, he looked into the other man's eyes before reaching out and curling a hand before his chin. Jay drew him closer, savouring the moment and the gentle touch, before giving him the gentlest of kisses.

Dominic's fingers curled beneath his chin and inched Jay closer. "You are so fuckin' beautiful. Open your eyes and let me me see 'em."

With his lips still sealed against Dominic's, Jay did as he was asked. The other man's dark eyes stared back at him and he felt Dominic gasp. Those long fingers crept from beneath his chin to cradle his cheek.

"So beautiful. I've never seen eyes so blue. They're like a spring day. Or the ocean."

Jay blushed and moved to lower his head. He was stopped by Dominic's hand cupping his jaw.

"Don't. I want to look at you as I kiss you."

He felt a bashful smile tug at his lips and, when Dominic moved him closer, Jay couldn't help himself. He gave himself over to Dominic, falling into the other man's arms and allowing Dominic to tend to his wounded soul.

The couch shifted as Dominic moved to straddle his lap. Thick, muscular thighs slid along his own and strong hands clasped the back of his head. Jay groaned as the dark-haired man pressed himself close. Dominic's arousal was obvious through his black jeans. Their kiss deepened and Jay pushed himself deeper into the couch. His hands slid around the other man's waist, his fingers finding hints of love handles before sliding up Dominic's broad back. He welcomed Dominic closer and encouraged him. The feeling of having someone close awakened something deep inside of Jay. Along with the lust he could feel old habits being to rise.

With his head swimming, he pulled away and rested his head on Dominic's shoulder. His breath came in short, sharp pants.

"Sorry," he whispered.

Dominic's hands still petted his hair as though trying to reassure him. "It's okay."

He gently stroked Dominic's back. "It's not." Jay sighed and hugged Dominic. He didn't want to let him go. Didn't want the other man to suddenly walk out of his life. They'd come so far together and he didn't want his own stupidity to ruin it. "There's certain things that still come up. I had – still do have – a sex addiction. It nearly ruined my marriage several times before I ruined it myself by coming out of the closet. You're not a toy, Dominic. You're not here to be used for my pleasure. I refuse to go down that route. I want to, dare I say it-" He paused and let a soft breath whisper over Dominic's neck. "fall in love with you rather than use you. Sorry..."

"What are you sorry for?" Dominic shifted and sat back on his heels. One hand still rested in the small of Jay's neck while the other reached for his face. Dominic's thumb swept over his cheek and there was a look of gentle admiration on his face. "You have nothing to be sorry for. I'm not here just for a good time, Jay. I'm here for as long as you'll have me. And you saying what you've said... Damn, that's a whole lot of reassurance for me right there. Like I said to you the other day, so many people here just want short term relationships. I'm too damn old for that." His lips whispered across Jay's cheek. "I want to wake up next to someone for a very long time."

Jay couldn't help himself. His arms once more locked around Dominic's waist and he held the dark-haired man close. Arms thick with muscles and decorated with tattoos slid around around his neck.

"I'll be here when you wake," he said. "I promise."

Chapter 10

Jay woke with a cold sense of dread in his heart. The bed itself also seemed to mirror that feeling. On opening his eyes, Jay found that the spot that had been occupied by Dominic was now empty and cold to the touch. The dark-haired man had, however, been replaced by a very happy and very excited cat.

"Where'd your friend go, huh?" He scratched Blue's head and, as the cat shifted, Jay spotted something scrunched up beneath his front paws.

Giving Blue a nudge, Jay pulled out a piece of paper. He unfolded it and smiled as he read the other man's capitalised handwriting.

Don't panic. Gone out. Be back soon. D x

The ache in his heart melted away and, for a moment, Jay stared at the words that Dominic had left. For Jay, as someone who'd locked themselves away for so very long, they meant something. They were a sign that someone was thinking about him and the insecurities that still sadly lived in his soul. Jay had told Dominic about how he suffered with abandonment issues and how the sex and alcohol addictions were linked to those. To wake up alone and cold when there had been someone present just a few hours earlier was enough to set the broken program in his brain running once more. But to wake up and find a note helped to stop that process before it had time to take hold.

Jay hauled himself from bed and fed the cat before starting to fix breakfast. There was a knock at the door just as the coffee machine was starting to bubble.

Still dressed in his pyjamas, Jay went and answered.

Standing in the doorway was a busy green fir tree. The sweet, nostalgic scent of its sap instantly hit his nose and Jay leaned against the door frame.

"Move. Move. Move. It's freezing out here and this thing's heavy." The tree's branches shook as Dominic tried to squeeze both himself and the tree past Jay and into the house.

"What did I say about decorations?"

"You didn't want any." Dominic peered around the branches. "But this is a tree. It's useful. You can burn it afterwards and the house will smell great."

There was going to be no arguing with Dominic and Jay decided to allow himself to lose the Battle of the Tree. Stepping to one side, he watched with a smirk as Dominic waddled inside with the tree clutched to his chest. His car sat out on the snow-covered driveway with a rear door open. Jay could see a box on the back seat.

"What's in the back of your car?"

"Tree stand and lights." Dominic panted as he leaned the tree against the stone wall before doubling over to catch his breath. His cold-reddened hands clasped his knees as he panted and his hair was held back by his thick-rimmed glasses. "Lights are from when I had the barbecue. Used to put 'em on the gazebos." Dominic took another shuddering breath. "I'm too old for this shit."

Dominic finally straightened up, took the glasses from his head, and shook his hair out. Jay looked at him, then at the tree, before turning back to Dominic. The corner of his mouth twitched upward. "So why a tree?"

"You sure ask a lot of questions. You need a hobby, Hammond. Maybe take up playing guitar again. It'll be good for you," the other man finished with a smirk. "Now give me a hand putting this tree up."

It took them an hour to wrangle the tree into the stand and drape its branches with lights. Nestled in the corner with just white lights for decoration, Jay had to admit that the tree looked good.

"Christmas returned to Christmas Cottage," Dominic said cheerfully. "Now I need a coffee and to get back to work."

Rolling his eyes, Jay grinned. "Want breakfast to go with that? I was going to make oatmeal."

Dominic waved his hands over his slightly rounded figure and gave Jay a cheeky smile. "Does this body look like it's allergic to food? Of course I want feeding! Hauling that tree around really took it out of me."

Squeezed into the tiny kitchen with Dominic and Blue, Jay made coffee and stoneware bowls of hot oatmeal. He sprinkled winter berries and drizzled honey on the breakfast dish before handing one to Dominic. The dark-haired man promptly began shovelling it into his mouth and swallowed each spoonful with an appreciative groan. Jay smiled before savouring his own breakfast. Having someone to share breakfast with really was an improvement on the previous months of his life.

"So what are you doing for Christmas?" Dominic scraped the inside of the bowl. The sound set Jay's teeth on edge but he said nothing.

"Nothing," he replied with a shrug. "Going to spend it here with the cat."

"Same. Except no cat. Well, spend it alone in the apartment. Probably watching old movies and eating garbage from the store."

Jay wasn't sure if Dominic was making conversation or vying for somewhere to spend Christmas Day. The big day was less than seventy two hours away and, well...

He felt himself crack. "Do you want to come here? I can't promise that there'll be anything spectacular for dinner but it sure beats spending it alone."

Dominic stared at him with the last dregs of oatmeal halfway to his mouth. "I mean, you don't have to offer, Jay. I'm fine by myself." The other man sighed and licked his spoon clean. "But, yeah, some company would be nice. Thanks. I appreciate it."

"No worries." Jay smiled and leaned over to drop his bowl in the sink. "Christmas is supposed to be a time for people to get together. I know I said that I want to be left the fuck alone but you know what, Dominic?" Heaving himself onto the counter, Jay settled down to talk to the other man. "I came out of the closet for a reason. I was tired of living a lie. I know we've been over this a thousand times already but I keep needing to say it. I came out of the closet and went straight back to living the life of a recluse. I'm not a people person; most people's energy makes me feel off balance. It was one of the many reasons that I drank and fucked around; that was the only way for me to feel normal. But I still realise that I need to spend time with someone." He smiled softly.

"Especially if I kind of like them."

That was all it took for Dominic to cross the kitchen. He stood between Jay's parted knees and Jay found himself staring down into chocolate-brown eyes framed by midnight-dark hair. Streaks of grey were beginning to work their way through Dominic's hair and beard and wrinkles curled from the corners of his eyes. He'd obviously spent years laughing and smiling and nothing seemed to have slowed him down.

He took a lock of Dominic's hair and tucked it behind the other man's ear. For that moment he savoured the silence and the gentle touches, just enjoying being in Dominic's warm and caring presence.

"Go and open the shop," he said softly. "See who comes and visits today. And, once your day's over, there'll be a meal waiting for you here."

Dominic's smile was full of love and warmth. Jay leaned down and gave him the gentlest of kisses as though determined to steal the smile for himself.

❄❄❄

Where there had once been a day of eating junk food and reading in front of the fire, there was now one that required a fully cooked meal. With that in mind, Jay bundled himself into warm clothes and made his way to the store. Snow crunched beneath his feet and tumbled from the branches above his head.

The store was busy, just as he'd thought it would be. Everyone – from locals to those who were visiting for the Christmas period – were shopping. Putting his head down, Jay wandered from aisle to aisle, picking up bits and pieces as he went. A turkey, vegetables, sauces, dessert... All of it went into the wire basket that hung from his elbow.

Pausing to catch himself amid the pre-Christmas chaos, Jay found himself standing on the personal hygiene aisle. His eyes swept over shampoo, conditioner, toothpaste, and all manner of other products before falling onto the tiny boxes of condoms. Slender bottles of lube sat beside them.

Jay didn't give himself time to even question what was going through his head. Reaching out, he grabbed one of each and tossed them into the basket.

❄❄❄

In his previous life, back when he'd been married, Jay had been a hunter. It had been his own version of field to fork, taking only what he needed from the land and preparing it himself. While he'd remained in the same state that he'd lived while married, he'd yet to take advantage of the local hunting.

Cooking had a similar effect on him, relaxing and focusing his mind as he worked through the steps of preparing a dish.

His phone chimed at his elbow and Jay glanced down to see a message from Clara.

Your photo is online. No identifying details. Just your music and your cat (that no-one knows you have. You should show him off more. He's gorgeous!). Next stage of Make Dominic Money will go live in the New

Year. Merry Christmas! C xx

Jay grinned and sent her a quick reply. Normally he bought Christmas gifts for everyone. But as he'd not been feeling in the mood, he'd handed the task to a specialist gift buying company and asked them to play Santa. He just hoped that the band's staff would like whatever they were gifted.

The smell of thick, meaty soup filled the tiny cottage. Jay had already cleaned the grate and laid a new fire. Bread was baking in the oven and Blue was dozing on the stairs with one paw poking through the bannister lest Jay forgot that he existed.

A car pulled up while Jay was laying the table and he moved to answer the door. The tree's lights were on and casting tiny stars on the darkened glass of the window.

Dominic stepped from his car and opened the trunk. He pulled out the two radiators and began dragging one through the snow before Jay moved to help him.

"Heating oil's arrived."

"How's the shop?" Jay pulled the first radiator inside before returning for the second one.

"Jumping. Seriously. So many last minute Christmas shoppers have been coming in. I'm going to open super early tomorrow and stay open later."

Satisfaction warmed Jay and he gave Dominic a small nod as he heaved the second radiator inside. Good had come from their slightly bizarre friendship.

"I'm glad it's getting better." A wolfish grin crossed his lips as he turned to watch Dominic closing the front door. "Did you check Winter Angels' social media pages today?"

Dominic looked at him with his coat dangling down his back and one arm still hooked in a sleeve. "No. Why?"

"Just... Maybe you should." Jay's grin widened and he turned back to the kitchen. "Make yourself comfortable. Dinner will be out in a moment."

There was a change in the air, a tension, and Jay couldn't help smiling as he filled bowls with soup and piled plates with bread.

"HOLY FUCKING SHIT! WHAT?! Jay, are you fucking for real?!"

He nonchalantly slid two bowls onto the table before looking at Dominic. "It's there, isn't it?"

Dominic turned his phone around so that Jay could see the page. And there it was, the photograph that he'd taken of Blue chilling beside a couple of Winter Angels sheet music books. The caption read *Just chilling at Between the Sheets (speciality sheet music store) in Waybridge, Colorado.*

There were already several thousand reactions to the post and Jay felt the warmth return once more. "You're doing good."

"I wouldn't be doing this well without you." Dominic's voice was soft and touched with tears. "Thank you."

Reaching out, Jay touched a hand to Dominic's face. He looked down into the other man's eyes and took in the bitter-sweet happiness that swept through them. For a moment his heart ached. "Maybe our paths were meant to cross like this. Maybe that's what all of this was for."

"Maybe." Dominic sighed and leaned into his touch. "Or maybe it's because we're two souls who were meant to find one another."

Leaning down, Jay pressed a kiss to Dominic's forehead. "Eat your soup before it gets cold. You're gonna need your strength for tomorrow."

Chapter 11

Christmas Eve. Jay hadn't dared to think that he would be out of the house on such a day. He'd imagined being stretched out on the couch with Blue on his knees and a book in his hands. He hadn't thought that he'd be weaving in and out of the crowds that were cluttering up Main Street.

He wasn't going to complain; the air was crisp and clear, the skies were blue, and the scenery was fantastic. A brass band played Christmas carols beneath the town's famous six-faced clock. Every shop was hopping with people and those who weren't rushing for gifts were soaking up the atmosphere outside of coffee shops and restaurants.

There was no way Dominic could spend Christmas with him without getting a gift. Both of them were alone and, while it seemed like Dominic had spent many Christmases alone, Jay knew that the sight of a gift beneath a tree made a person feel that little more loved and welcomed. And Dominic had done so much for him over the previous weeks. Dominic would argue that Jay had done more for him. But where he'd provided some material support to Dominic, the dark-haired man had taught Jay himself how to come out of his bubble and break down his barriers. He was learning to love and care for another again.

He was passing by the Book Nook when a thought crossed his mind. Pausing, Jay thought over the first time they'd met and Dominic's dismissal of his reading material. He ducked into the shop and found that there were several other people already browsing the shelves.

Book Nook was the epitome of quaint. Like every other shop on the street, it had a high vaulted ceiling that had been left bare in order to show off its rafters. Dark wood bookcases lined every wall and several more created narrow aisles in the centre of building. A cluttered cashier's desk was pushed to one side and an elderly woman smiled as he walked in.

"Are you looking for anything in particular?"

Jay shook his head. "I'm just browsing, thanks."

There was that wonderful smell of printed paper, a smell that bought a sense of safety and solitude. All Jay could think about was sitting in front of the fire on Christmas night with Dominic's feet in his lap and a book in his own hands. Wistfully, he wandered along the tiny aisles as he tilted his head to read the spines.

As with any bookshop, there was an array of different topics, all of them no doubt lovingly picked out by the owner and mirroring, to some degree, her passions.

He read about botany, cookery, true crime, and spirituality. The crick in his neck niggled yet he refused to listen to it. For the moment he was lost in the wonderful world of books.

Fairy lights were strung in the rafters and a Christmas tree decorated with ornaments made from old books stood in one corner. The shop, like every shop in Waybridge, was a perfect slice of what life should be like. Small town America at its finest.

Jay found himself rounding the shelves and returning to the cooking section. Dominic had left behind his previous barbecuing life but, from his figure and the way he put away food while under Jay's roof, Jay assumed that he still had an interest in food. Dominic seemed like the kind of guy who appreciated food no matter where it came from.

His eyes fell onto a book about Japanese cooking and Jay tugged it from the shelf. Titled *From the Locals*, it covered all of the main dishes. Dominic liked challenges; he'd said so himself, and a new cookbook seemed to be the perfect gift.

Tucking it beneath his arm, Jay made his way to the register. The desk was covered with little knick-knacks and Jay found himself swiping up a bookmark that was decorated with cookies and cakes.

The lady behind the counter smiled at him. "Did you find what you were looking for?"

Handing her the book, Jay replied, "I certainly hope so. It's a Christmas gift."

"Well, books sure make good gifts. Do you want it wrapping?"

He nodded. "Yes, please."

She turned away and began wrapping the book in Christmas themed brown paper while he reached for his wallet. Jay felt a sense of peace settle over him as he leaned on the counter and gazed at the shop. He really had made the right choice in coming out and moving away. The band would always be there and, even if he never returned he had, as Dominic had said, left a huge legacy behind.

And Dominic. The guy he'd met at Joe's who'd started out as a fan and quickly stolen Jay's heart. He was sweet and gentle and funny and oh-so-lovable. Jay loved seeing him smile. And loved waking up to see those dark, doe eyes staring back at him. And Dominic had never once tried to pry into his life or push him to go back to making music. He just wanted someone to hang out with, talk to, and hopefully fall in love with.

"Here you go, dear."

Jay turned to find the lady holding a paper bag. He smiled and took it from her before handing over his credit card. She swiped it and gave him the receipt to sign. Jay wanted to get going but a sudden thought popped into his head.

"Have you ever been to Between the Sheets?" he asked.

"The music store up the road? Yes. Why?"

Jay let the bag rest on the counter top. "The guy that runs it, Dominic, what's he like?"

The lady's face broke into a huge, warm smile. "He's been in here a few times. Such a sweetheart. Originally from Virginia by way of California, I believe. Why'd you ask?"

"No real reason." Jay shrugged. "My company's doing some work for him, that's all."

"Well, you look after him. That boy's been through some tough times."

Jay's smile was soft and almost apologetic. "I gathered." He swept up the bag and hooked it over his wrist. "Thanks, and Merry Christmas."

"Merry Christmas! You have a good one."

Main Street was still busy and Jay ducked into Joe's to pick up a couple of take out coffees. The fire was roaring and people were finding a little respite from the bitter winter air. As he waited in line, Jay overheard snippets of conversation. People were talking about incoming snow, and the coming holidays, and being with family. Jay felt their love and warmth and allowed himself to bask in it. He was finally allowing himself to start the new life that he'd dreamed of for so long. A life that was small and cosy and filled with love.

Between the Sheets was as busy as the street outside. People were flicking through the bookcases and Dominic seemed to have a constant stream of customers. No sooner had he rung up one than another person appeared at the desk.

Slipping through the crowd, Jay popped a cup in front of Dominic before walking behind the counter. "You ring them up and I'll bag them."

"You'll be recognised," Dominic hissed.

"Don't care. I'll say I'm here on vacation." He smiled as an older lady stepped up to the counter. "Morning, ma'am."

For the next three hours they rang up and bagged purchases. Credit cards were swiped and cash changed hands. Despite Dominic's warning, Jay found that he only had to sign a single autograph and didn't have to explain why he was bagging sheet music in a tiny Colorado town.

Darkness had fallen over Waybridge by the time the last customer inched their way out of the shop. Dominic was leaning on the counter with a look of triumphant resignation on his face. Lifting the keys from beside the register, Jay went and quietly locked the door.

"Dinner?" he softly asked.

Dominic pulled himself onto his elbows. "Let me et it tonight. You came here with coffee and gave me a hand. You didn't have to do that. What would you like? Pizza? Steak?" A wicked twinkle danced through Dominic's eyes. "Me?"

Chuckling softly, Jay made his way back to the counter and brushed the hair from Dominic's eyes. "Pizza sounds good. And then you if I'm not too full."

Resting his elbows in front of Dominic's, Jay's leaned in and gave the other man a kiss. He felt Dominic purr against his lips before shifting a little closer.

"We also need to talk," Jay softly continued.

"Ugh." Dominic playfully rolled his eyes. "I hate that line. What do you want to talk about?"

He gave Dominic a soft smile as he looked into the other man's dark eyes. "I need routine. You've probably worked that out by now. And you've become a part of that routine quite quickly. I enjoy being around you and cooking for you. But I need to know where we stand with one another. Are we friends? Or...?" His voice trailed off.

Dominic frowned and his brown eyes seemed to get a little darker. For a heartbeat, Jay felt worry flicker through him. "Well, considering I've woken up next to you for the past few days, and even though I've yet to see you naked, which is driving me insane by the way because, *damn*, that body's hot as hell, I'd say that we're in a relationship. Is that what you need to hear."

Pressing his forehead to Dominic's, Jay nodded and gave him a wistful smile. "That's exactly what I needed to hear. Thank you."

"Is that what you wanted to talk about?"

"That's exactly what I wanted to talk about." He gave Dominic's nose a kiss before straightening up and finding his coat. "And, on that note, I think we should go and find pizza before everything closes up for the next day or so."

Chapter 12

Main Street's clientele had changed, the shoppers having given way to Christmas bar-hoppers and hungry store owners. Jay thought back on the times when he'd have happily joined those staggering from bar to bar and drowned the Christmas spirit with as much alcohol as possible.

Wrapped up against the cold, they walked amid the throngs of people. No one stopped them. No one asked for photos or autographs. It was almost as though the town was allowing Jay to integrate and become one of them.

Gloved fingers brushed his own and Jay discreetly laced his hand with Dominic's. Their talk, no matter how brief it had been, had helped to alleviate his fears that Dominic had been looking for someone to keep him warm during the winter only to disappear once spring arrived. Dominic seemed to be in it for the long haul and, for that, Jay was eternally grateful. His heart felt full and his soul sang a new, and happy, song.

Mario's stood at the very top of Main Street. On one side of it was an Italian restaurant while there was nothing but the open vista of the mountains and trees on the other. The road was pedestrianised, permanently closed to cars in order to allow tourists and locals to move freely along the town's shopping street. Parking was ample and free, something that Jay was planning on taking advantage of once he'd regained his license. Meeting Dominic had woken many things inside of him, including thoughts of what he wanted to do with Christmas Cottage. The garden was the first on an expansive list of DIY projects and, for that, he was going to need to haul himself to the garden centre just off the main thoroughfare.

Fairy lights were strung in the window of the pizza parlour and a small plastic tree sat in one corner of the counter. Dominic's fingers squeezed Jay's as they approached the door.

"What would you like?"

Instinctively, Jay reached for his wallet. "I've got this."

"No, Hammond, you haven't. I already said that I've got this." Dominic grinned at him in the glow of the fairy lights, his eyes twinkling with festive specks of colour. "Let me spoil you for once. What do you want?"

Jay shrugged. "Anything with meat on it – pepperoni?"

Dominic's face was adorable in the street's soft lights. His smile was a mile wide and his eyes were as dark as the sky above them. He seemed so happy to be with someone and making them happy in return. Jay's hand left Dominic's and the dark-haired man moved to squeeze into the busy take out.

"You gonna wait out here or-"

"I'll wait out here."

Truth be told, Jay was enjoying the crisp coldness of the evening air. The sky was full of stars and the stark chill held the promise of more snow. Letting Dominic go, Jay propped himself on a nearby planter and leaned back to admire the heavens above him. His own childlike wonder crept out as his eyes tracked first a satellite and then a shooting star. The debate as to whether they were alone in the universe was one as old as time and Jay suspected that it was the kind of topic that would excite Dominic's inquisitive mind. The other man had done so much in his life; musician, chef, business owner, store owner, music lover... and Jay suspected that he enjoyed deep discussions.

"Asking the universe questions, huh?" Dominic's gentle voice caught him off guard and Jay brought himself back to Earth. The dark-haired man had two pizza boxes clasped in his hands and a plastic bag slung over one elbow.

Looking at Dominic, he nodded. "Something like that, yes. How long have you been gone?"

He shrugged. "Fifteen minutes, maybe. I stood in the shop and watched you watch the sky." Dominic's smile was soft in the gentle light. "You were really enamoured with what you were looking at. It was nice to watch."

Jay wasn't going to lie; Dominic was melting every brick of the ice wall that he'd originally built around himself. Love, he'd suspected, should have come from somewhere else; an app that he dared not use, or a blind date set up by a friend. Never did he think that some random guy who'd plonked themselves next to him in a crowded coffee shop would capture his heart in such a way.

His own voice was soft as he replied, "Thanks."

Dominic just gave him a smile before nudging him with an elbow. Nothing needed to be said as they made their way back along the street and towards the tiny cottage with the roaring fire.

✣✣✣

Jay groaned as he sank back into the couch and rested a hand on his full stomach. The coffee table was littered with open boxes, cans of soda, and plates that could wait until morning before being washed. Blue was curled up on the rug before the fire having feasted on whatever the two men couldn't finish.

There was a soft moan from beside him and Jay turned his head to look at Dominic. The dark-haired man was all but stretched out, his head back against the couch's pillows and his eyes closed. His hands rested on his slightly swollen stomach.

"That's some damn good pizza."

"Yeah. Haven't been there before," Jay said. "Always cooked for myself."

A dark eye cracked open and Dominic gave him a crooked smile. "There's other places I could introduce you to. That Italian place. Another Mexican place on the other side of the river. Damn, I love me some Mexican."

Glancing at Dominic's shirt, Jay nodded. The other man's black tshirt had the words *Tacos, burritos, enchiladas, and nachos* stencilled on it. It was almost as though Dominic was carrying around his own personal food order just in case he should happen upon a Mexican restaurant.

"Well, there's turkey and all the trimmings for dinner tomorrow. Hopefully that'll be okay for you."

Dominic snorted and rolled his head against the back of the couch. "Okay? Hammond, I don't know if you've noticed but this body ain't allergic to food. You cook it, I'll eat it. Shit, I wish I still had my smoker. Would have been great to put the turkey on there."

"Why don't we get you one in the new year?" Jay felt his heart clench at the suggestion. He'd promised himself that he wouldn't treat Dominic like a charity case and here he was offering up new barbecue gear. For all he knew, Dominic wanted to be completely away from the barbecue scene.

Those eyes, the ones that looked like melted chocolate, opened to look at him. Dominic's face was so soft and so earnest that Jay felt any worry he had vanish. "Seriously?"

He nodded. "Yeah. Seriously. You tell me what you want and I'll get it shipped out here. Call it my Christmas gift to you. 'Cause I've got a feeling you're not doing much cooking in that apartment."

"You're right, I'm not." Dominic wrinkled his nose. "Don't get me wrong; I'm not complaining. But the kitchen is basic. Electric oven and an electric hob. There's only so much you can do with that. You ever go cooking on campfires?"

"All the time." Jay smiled softly at the memories of his younger self. Stretching his legs out, he draped one ankle over the other. "I'm going to do the garden once the summer's here. You're making me think about putting a fire pit out there."

"Sounds like a good plan. It'll be nice to sit around come fall. That's if you keep me around, of course. 'Cause I'm sure I'm gonna piss you off at some point."

Laughing, Jay shook his head. "I'm not going to get rid of you."

"Fuck," Dominic breathed. "You lose like twenty

years when you laugh. Like, seriously, I've never seen someone taken over so completely when they laugh. It's beautiful."

They fell quiet and the silence was warm and relaxing. Jay allowed himself to fall into it, the warmth becoming the blanket that he so desperately needed. He knew that there was so much more that he needed to do with Dominic. Opening up, laying his soul bare, not dictating how things worked between them. Dominic was as equal as he was and rehab and addictions need not be an excuse to having a fulfilling relationship.

Lips brushed his cheek and a hand came to rest on his chest. Opening an eye, Jay smiled at Dominic. The dark-haired man had shifted a little closer and was curling himself up on the couch. Lifting his arm, Jay draped it around Dominic's shoulder and pulled him closer. His lips found the parting of the other man's hair and gave it a gentle kiss.

This was what he'd wanted all along; someone to love and care for. Someone who accepted him for who he was.

With his head resting on top of Dominic's, Jay quietly watched the fire. His hand stroked over the other man's shoulder and he could feel Dominic's breath on his neck. An arm was slung over his chest, Dominic's fingers curled into the fabric of his shirt.

Curled together, they sat in silence. Blue eventually joined them and settled in a small gap between the two men. Jay couldn't help but smile at the cat's easy acceptance of the change in their home life. Blue seemed as happy with Dominic as Jay was.

Eventually the fire began to burn low. Jay checked his watch. 11.25pm.

"Nearly Christmas," he whispered.

"Mmm-hmm." Dominic was dozing, his weight heavy against Jay.

"Bed?"

"Sounds great."

Untangling themselves from the couch, the two men made their way to the stairs. For once there was no cat racing them to the bed and Jay paused to look back at the couch. Blue had stretched himself out in the warm spots that were left behind.

"Staying there?"

The cat flicked an ear and curled his legs beneath himself.

"Okay. See you once the couch has cooled down."

Butterflies swarmed in his stomach. It had been many years since they'd last made an appearance and Jay felt almost giddy at the prospect of spending another night sleeping next to someone. As he changed into flannel pyjamas, he couldn't help but steal glimpses of Dominic.

The dark-haired man seemed blissfully unaware that he was being watched. Instead, he stripped off without a care in the world. His glasses were discarded onto the dresser at the end of the bed. Pale skin that was etched with tattoos appeared from beneath the layers of denim and flannel.

Jay heard himself speak so softly he feared that his voice would disappear. "Dominic?"

The other man looked up from folding his jeans and gave Jay a gentle smile. "Yeah?"

He couldn't help himself. Stepping up to Dominic, he placed a hand on the dark-haired man's shoulder. His fingers grazed over naked skin, marvelling in its smoothness before sliding down over the muscular bulge of Dominic's upper arm.

"You're beautiful," he murmured.

Dominic didn't so much as blush. Instead his smile grew wider and his eyes sparkled with happiness. Jay's hand crept back along Dominic's arm until it was winding into the ends of his hair.

"Do you mind?"

Dominic gave a gentle shake of his head. "Not at all."

His breath hitched in his throat as his hands continued to wander over Dominic's body. Jay wanted to savour the moment, to lose himself in it, and commit every second to memory. He wanted to remember how Dominic felt beneath his touches, where his skin was smooth or aged, and the tiny sighs of pleasure that uttered from Dominic's lips.

Their kiss may have been gentle but it was filled with the kind of passion that Jay had always hoped it would be. He could feel himself growing more confident as his hands slide along Dominic's back and he pulled the other man to him. Dominic moaned softly and wrapped his arms around Jay's neck.

"This feels so good," Dominic murmured. "I love being here with you."

Jay smiled nervously. "And I love having you here. Thank you for spending Christmas with us."

In just a few short days his life had changed beyond all recognition and Jay felt his heart swell at the love that Dominic was lavishing on him. Never had he imagined that someone would be so open and honest with him and, in return, he silently promised that he'd do more of the same.

Once they had finally fallen into bed, he took Dominic in his arms and pulled the blankets over them. The dark-haired man smiled at him and Jay felt himself fall a little harder for him.

"Gonna be here when I wake up?"

Dominic leaned in and pressed a kiss to his nose. "There's food in the fridge, right?"

"Yeah."

"Then you can guarantee that I'll be here when you wake up." When Jay's expression became a little crestfallen, Dominic shuffled himself closer. "But there's honestly nowhere else I want to be. Merry Christmas, Jay."

Glancing over his shoulder, Jay looked to the clock beside the bed. 00.35.

"Merry Christmas, Dominic."

Chapter 13

"Merry Christmas!"

Jay looked up from the potatoes that he was peeling to find Dominic, dressed in his thickest winter coat, leaning against the kitchen entrance. He had a huge smile on his lips and that playful twinkle was back in his eyes.

"What are you up to, Dominic?" Placing the peeler to one side, Jay wiped his hands on his jeans and rested his weight against the counter. "You got up early and disappeared. Just like you said you wouldn't," he jokingly finished.

Dominic's smile somewhere widened even further and he pulled the knitted hat from his head. "Went to check on the shop and pick something up from the apartment. Come and take a look."

Jay waved a hand at the pile of vegetables on the counter. "But dinner-"

"But come on."

Dominic was insistent, Jay would give him that and, with a soft sigh, he followed the other man through to the living area. Blue was curled up in front of the fire, one ear flicking in the hope that what was coming through was food. When it wasn't, the cat settled back down with his nose tucked into his paws.

On the table lay a long black case. Jay eyed it suspiciously before looking to Dominic.

"What's this?"

Dominic shrugged and shoved his hands into the pockets of his coat. "It's gonna need to warm up. It's been in the apartment and then the car. I'd be careful for a couple of hours."

"Dominic?"

"Don't Dominic me!" the other man gently huffed. "Just open it!"

Staring at the case, Jay sighed and shook his head. "I'm not sure that I'm ready..."

"You don't have to be ready. But it'll be here for when you are."

Taking a deep breath, Jay hooked his fingers around familiar silver latches and flicked them up with a satisfying click. His hands paused on the black lid, his heart hammering at a million miles a minute. He knew what was in the case but wasn't sure if he was ready to face it.

"I don't know..."

"Take that wall down, Jay," Dominic murmured. "You can do it. One brick at a time."

Deep down, he knew that Dominic was right. Not wanting to see what was in the case was another wall that was stopping him from living his full life. Hell, it was stopping him from living the life that he'd been put on the planet for. Jay had walked away from everything he loved, including music, to try and fashion a new life out of what was left of his old self.

The hinges creaked slightly as he lifted the lid and tears prickled his eyes as he looked at the object nestled within the black velvet.

The guitar was a beautiful sandy colour with strings that looked as though they'd never been played. A single yellow guitar pick had been jammed beneath the strings. Jay felt his breath catch and he ran his fingers over the smooth, vanished wood.

"Dominic..."

"You don't have to play it right now. But it's there for when the urge returns." Dominic sounded a million miles away, a voice from a distant planet. All Jay could do was stare at the guitar in wonder and hope that, one day, he'd feel the need to pick it up and play.

Carefully, he closed the lid and, for a moment, allowed his hands to rest on the wood. All that was in the case was him. His life, his soul. It ran through his blood and lived in his heart. Turning his back on music had shattered him in ways that he could never have imagined. But he'd needed the break. He'd needed to walk away for a while and focus on finding himself. And now that he had...

Jay turned and smiled at Dominic. "Thank you. Really. Thank you."

Dominic looked at him with a worried expression and his hands clasped before him. "You like it?"

"I love it."

He wasn't sure that Dominic was buying his gratitude. Stepping up to Dominic, Jay gently wound a hand into the other man's waves of long, dark hair and pulled him in for a kiss. Arms draped around his waist and Dominic purred against him.

❄❄❄

True to his word, Dominic proved to be a whiz in the kitchen and, before long, dinner was almost ready. Leaving Dominic to finish the last of the side dishes, Jay went to lay the table. In the madness of cooking, he'd forgotten that the guitar case was lying in the centre of the dinner table.

It was pure instinct for his hand to wrap around the handle and heave the case up. A movement so natural that Jay didn't even think about what he was doing until the case was standing in a corner. Only then did he pause to look at the black case, the Christmas tree's fairy lights barely registering on its matte surface.

Once more his heart twinged and Jay reached out and ran a hand over the case. His fingers swept over the rough pattern of the protective fabric. The guitar was beautiful, there was no questioning that, and Jay wondered how Dominic had come by it. An impulse purchase from his new rush of customers? Or something he'd carried with him from his previous life?

"Probably about five minutes left on these sides," Dominic called from the kitchen. "Want me to start bringing food through?"

Stepping away from the guitar, Jay opened the cupboard and began gathering the table settings. He hadn't planned on going all out and decorating but, at the very least, he could make it look nice. So out came the place mats, and the nice glasses, and the cutlery that he'd impulse bought and never used. Out came the table runner whose origin he couldn't remember, and the candles, and the candelabra that desperately needed a polish.

Jay took a moment to admire the set up. Basic it may have been, but with only flickering candles and the tree for light, it was warm and homely. He stepped over the cat and stoked the fire, tossing on an extra log for good measure. Blue looked up at him and gave a soft meow before stretching out. Bending down, Jay scratched the cat's head.

"You'll get some turkey soon, sweetie."

The cottage was filled with the rich smells of a wonderful Christmas dinner. Making his way back into the kitchen, Jay found Dominic spooning vegetables into dishes.

"I was just gonna put them straight on the plate," Jay said.

Dominic shrugged and used a cloth to pick up two bowls. "Tough. They're already in bowls. Let's go, Hammond. I'm hungry."

Jay couldn't help but smile and shake his head. Dominic, and his forever-empty stomach, were turning into a source of amusement. Picking up some of the other food items, Jay followed him to the table.

Blue, just like Dominic, was another creature with a permanently-empty stomach. He'd already taken his place at the table, sitting himself neatly on a chair as though patiently waiting for a plate to be put before him.

"Cat doesn't eat at-" Jay waved a hand in Blue's general direction. "Ah, fuck it. Cat eats Christmas dinner at the table."

The table was soon covered with an array of foods. Some of them Jay was sure that he hadn't bought and wondered if someone had secreted them into the house, and then the oven, without being seen. At the heart of the vast spread was the turkey.

He looked to Dominic. "Want to do the honours?"

"Sure."

He watched as Dominic expertly went to work on the roasted meat. Blue, ever the scavenger, was leaning on the table until Jay gently nudged him back into his chair. Slivers of rich, juicy meat were carefully dropped onto plates. Seating himself at the table, Jay began to help himself to the bowls of colourful vegetables. The fire crackled behind him and he felt his shoulders slump as the stress melted out of them.

He added a few more pieces to Blue's little plate before covering it in gravy and placing it in front of the expectant-looking cat. Once Dominic had made himself comfortable, the cat tucked straight in. Jay smiled softly and scratched Blue's head before looking to Dominic.

Sunlight was still streaming through the window with bright rays of light bouncing off another load of freshly fallen snow. What would have been another normal day for Jay had turned into something something completely, and unexpectedly, different. In just a few short weeks, his life had gone from the monotony that he'd been craving but growing bored of to having someone bring joy and hope to a life that had otherwise been less than ordinary.

Picking up his cutlery, he smiled softly at Dominic. "This looks great."

"You did most of it. I just disappeared out to get the pieces that were at the apartment."

The small, vaulted room was soon filled with the soft sounds of two men thoroughly enjoying what would otherwise have been a long, and possibly lonely, day. They chatted back and forth and ignored the dirty dishes. Jay muttered something about them waiting until the following morning as he heaved himself from the table and to the couch. Taking a detour passed the Christmas tree, he picked up Dominic's gift before dropping himself onto the couch's overstuffed cushions. He waited until Dominic had joined him before handing out the gift-wrapped book.

"It's not much..."

"You didn't have to..." Dominic sat beside him and carefully began to unpick the red twine and star-decorated brown paper.

Jay's voice was as soft as his heart as he watched Dominic. He was fascinated by the other man. Fascinated by his gentleness, and love, and general admiration for life around him. Fascinated by how easily he'd fallen in love and given his heart to another. "I did."

Dominic gave him a gentle smile as the paper spread across his lap. The pleasant silence was broken by Dominic's suddenly-animated squeal of joy. He held the book before his face and turned it, admiring the sharp edges and crisp photography. The cover had a close up of a colourful dish.

"This is amazing! Thank you!"

"You like it?" Jay asked.

The dark-haired man leaned in until his forehead was resting against Jay's. "Of course I do. Thank you."

Lips found his and Dominic's free hand wound into the nap of his neck, pulling him closer. The butterflies that came to life whenever Dominic touched him once more took flight and Jay reached out to clasp Dominic's face, his thumbs resting on the swell of the other man's cheeks as their kiss deepened. Darkness had taken over the outside but, in the warmth of the cottage, a different kind of light had flickered to life.

Christmas had finally returned to Christmas Cottage.

Printed in Great Britain
by Amazon